Abou

James Fitzmaurice has written a number of award-winning screenplays. They include an imagined tale of a dream Barack Obama experiences in which he is plagued by the beat poet Charles Bukowski. In another screenplay, the novelist Raymond Carver navigates a love story while living in 1960s Iowa City, a place populated by Theory Zombies. In yet another script which is set in the 1660s, Margaret Cavendish (who lived in what became the Sheffield postal code area) tries to convince a famous religious writer that witches and devils do not exist. An ex-pat American himself, Jim taught at Northern Arizona University for many years before retiring to the UK, where has been associated with the University of Sheffield. The children he raised in Sheffield are now grown and have flown the nest. This is his first novel.

Hobgoblin Gennel

James Fitzmaurice

Hobgoblin Gennel

Vanguard Press

A CIP catalogue record for this title is
available from the British Library.

ISBN 978 1 83794 187 2

*Vanguard Press is an imprint of
Pegasus Elliot Mackenzie Publishers Ltd.*
www.pegasuspublishers.com

First Published in 2024

**Vanguard Press
Sheraton House Castle Park
Cambridge England**

Printed & Bound in Great Britain

To my family.

Gratitude to the family and friends who listened to me talk incessantly about this project. Special thanks to Anne Fitzmaurice Adams and Katherine Kwok for their practical suggestions.

PART ONE

Chapter 1

Walking to Millhouses Pond

Irie was actually fond of her little brother, but she was not about to play babysitter for him during the week of half-term break early in June. The school year in Sheffield didn't end until late-July, and half-term definitely provided relief from the academic work of Year 11. An additional boon this year lay in the fact that the pandemic, which had hit in March, was now thawing in the summer sun. Not gone, but not freezing life itself anymore. Fredrick Gustafson, American expat, best male friend and bubble mate, wanted to watch the RC boats on the pond in Millhouses Park. Irie preferred not to complicate the situation with a six-year-old boy in tow.

Irie spoke in a hush. "That's Mum with little brother Sanka... Off the pavement, Freddie, and into the shade of the lychgate." The rosy-cheeked sixteen-year-old Fred did not respond immediately, so Irie firmly pulled him by the sleeve of his Yuma Criminals tee-shirt from the sidewalk and into the space under the moss-covered lychgate. It was wooden in a sturdy way, but with a few shingles askew. If you looked carefully, the outlines of two runes could be seen on one of the side supports. Long ago in the Middle Ages, lychgates stood guard in front of churches, and they still did sometimes in the UK and in Sheffield in particular. But ordinary house owners liked to build them too – over driveways, not to ward off evil spirits but to give their houses what Irie jokingly called "that old timie feeling."

Fred did not mind occasionally being pulled this way and that, and his classmate Irie had probably saved his life a time or two when they crossed busy streets. He knew it. Or at least that was her considered opinion about both the facts and his knowledge of them.

He whispered, "Irie, these lychgates really belong over the foot paths that lead up to churches. Medieval architecture as a modern driveway ornament." She had heard this story from him before and knew he would go on until stopped.

Irie replied, "Shush."

A moment later, Mum wearing a blue paper COVID mask and little brother Sanka stood before the two friends. Stood and looked right through them.

Mum had a puzzled expression on her face. "I could've sworn that girl… I can almost smell her." Mum's voice had a wonderful lilt. Mum inherited it from Irie's nan, who had grown up in Jamaica.

Brother Sanka, being his usual self, was oblivious. "Why are we stopping? We're going shopping. I wanna go shopping."

Mum: "We'll get there. Don't go on about it."

Sanka: "Kinder Surprise?"

Mum: "So that's why you're keen to go to the shops. If you ask again, no Kinder Surprise. Otherwise maybe."

Mum and brother Sanka drifted into the distance. The two friends now stepped out from under the lychgate. Fred, however, caught his toe on the edge of the place where the driveway meets the sidewalk. He stumbled but steadied himself by reaching to the wooden lychgate support beam, his fingers just covering one of the two runes. Fred's face flushed red and he felt a tingle in his fingers. He turned his head to look at the rune, which he recognized as a thorn written "þ". Thorn was a letter for "th" in Anglo-Saxon. He knew this little piece of information from looking around in his father's books. It also showed up in his fantasy and sci-fi novels.

"How did they not see us?" he said, and he seemed befuddled.

"Beats me," responded Irie, returning him a wee twist of a smile.

Fred, as was his custom, changed the subject out of the blue: "I like it when your Mum wears a COVID mask . . . I used to love those little chocolate eggs with the surprise in the middle. The Kinder Surprise. Memories of childhood come flooding back."

Irie was used to Fred's combining disconnected statements and replied with some of her own. Irie: "Me and you both. We agree on wearing masks. Not so keen on childhood memories, at the moment. More interest in our starting A-Level work at High Storrs School in September. Remember, we're in a COVID bubble together, so don't need to wear masks when it's just the two of us." Irie giggled as she continued: "Your lost childhood. No more Kinder Surprises because you've grown ever so old."

He shot her one of his friendly rivalry looks. "All the bubble means is that if one person gets the plague then the other does, too . . . I remember when you would kill for a Kinder Surprise. Yeah, you too."

She shrugged. "Don't be difficult."

"It's 'you and I,' by the way. Not 'me and you,' like you said." Fred enjoyed correcting people's usage of the English language.

Irie: "What I put up with, hanging about with a grammar freak. We're only sixteen. We don't have A-Level exams for two years. Let's find our way to the RC boat pond that you're so fixated on."

Fred was amused: "'Fixated'? RC boat obsessive-compulsive disease. If anyone has it, I do. And 'Find our way'? No detours, please." He stopped himself from mentioning that she had ended a sentence with a preposition. She was, of course, a friend and being kind to friends is a good thing, even if she sometimes acted superior because she was a month older.

The two briskly proceeded down the street, encountering a red pillar post box along the way. There, cast into the metal, was a monogram that identified the reigning monarch of the time – E II R. That is, Elizabeth the second Regina. Fred gave a little run at the post box and swung himself around as if it were a pole. On they meandered in the balmy weather towards Millhouses Park and the RC pond.

Fred: "I love the British Isles, where a post box is in the form of a post."

Chapter 2

A Mathematics Boffin

When the clouds are not bucketing down rain as they often do in June, Millhouses pond is a good place to spend a few hours watching animals and people. Not just RC boats. Dogs chase Frisbees. Toddlers stumble around on the sweet-smelling grass. There are bird watchers and young lovers. Teenage boys and girls holding hands. Gay couples. Old folks, who once hurled brutal accusations at one another, slowly and carefully tread the paths, people now as placid as the pond itself.

One of the birdwatchers was the elderly Mr Simon Grasshwort, a member of the Geomancer Society in bad standing. A man who favoured wearing green corduroy trousers and who did not habitually keep his shoes free of mud, he showed clear signs of being unhappy. His status in the Society was not the cause of this dismay. Simply put, his wife Elaine had disappeared, not in the sense of slowly dissolving like a person being beamed up into a starship. Rather, she was not at home when he returned from a long set of errands and expected to see her sitting and reading under a yellow-fringed lamp. All that signalled her recent presence was a still-warm bread maker out on the granite kitchen counter. The warm bread maker was accompanied by a small empty bag of pre-mix flour for focaccia. Elaine had gone missing in the way that people sometimes do, but Simon was not one to file a report or to get the police involved in any way.

Simon did not dislike or mistrust the police. Rather, he had reason to believe that Elaine had been metamorphosed into a small woodland bird. He knew that as a person she frequented a place where wild garlic grows in June, and so he stood with a pair of binoculars looking across the River Sheaf into a wooded area where he thought she might go out of habit, though as a bird she could hardly pick garlic. He was reasonably sure that she was not now a robin that would brazenly confront him from newly turned soil in his garden. He thought she might be a wood pigeon, one that cooed on misty mornings. A bird that Fred, the American, would have called a dove (though Simon did not know Fred, even casually). More likely, perhaps, the transformation was into a house sparrow, the sort of bird that eats from what falls from the tables at outdoor restaurants. Simon was only sure that Elaine liked garlic that was not store bought. He and she had argued mightily before the transformation and it seemed possible to him that she was simply an old girl "gone wild," with substantial love for garlic still left over from her many years as a human being.

***

Fred's birthday took place two months after Irie's, and so he was, technically, younger. Clearly, Irie took too much delight in reminding him of this fact. He was, however, far more junior to his older sister, Melanie, who was eighteen and finishing up studying for A-Level exams at High Storrs School. A-Level scores were everything when it came to getting into college. "Getting into university" was what Irie would have said because she was English. It was helpful to have good grades in classes, but the final decision on who was going to which university in England in September of 2020 was based on a day of exams. What if you had the sniffles or just felt horrible on the appointed day? What if you sometimes totally freaked out in timed exams? Fred liked the American system better, the system that spread out the pain of getting grades over many classes. But his parents had plunked him down in Sheffield, and there was no undoing what had been done.

Fred's older sister, Melanie, now sat on the Millhouses lawn away from the pond and out of sight of Irie and Fred. Melanie, fearing grass stains on her jeans, was perched on her flattened backpack. Beside her was a pile of books including one that gave off an odour of mathematics. If the truth be known, Melanie was a math whiz, a "boffin" to her Sheffield classmates, but one of the nice ones, as her younger brother observed when he was making an effort to be nice himself. She twiddled a home-made COVID mask. Her classmate in year 13, Ralph Whitby-Smith, who liked to go by the name Rafe, sat across from her at the pandemic-safe distance of two meters. He had books with him and no mask in sight. Fred, as might be expected, disliked the numbering system for classes in high school in the UK. For him, year 13 should be year 12. But final year in secondary school would still be as sweet if it were year 12.5. It would still be top of the heap in spite of any worries about university or "real life" that might lurk in the background. Melanie inched forward towards Rafe.

"Rafe, what do you think? Are the teachers that are marking the A-level exams going to be tougher this year? I'd say so. Agree?" Melanie the math boffin spoke with a transatlantic accent, neither pure English nor pure American, but a mix. She did not sound much like her younger brother, whose accent would not have been noticed in the schoolrooms of Yuma or on the light rail of Phoenix. He sounded American without a doubt, while she had adapted to her new surroundings half-way around the world.

Rafe's speech was marked by its own sort of mix: a posh la-dee-da kind of English that was almost a parody of the English upper classes. He also sounded a little like Sheffield in an accent that came and went. When he heard what Melanie said about the A-Level exams, he continued fiddling with his cell phone for a few seconds and then looked up. "I'd give you odds that the teachers marking A-Level exams will come down on us hard. Like a ton of bricks. Last year they were too easy. There's always a pendulum with A-Levels and it's swinging the wrong way for me… For us. But you've got the gift of maths. You tell me the odds. Give me the numbers. The probabilities. Which reminds me. Have you done that abominable maths homework yet? The stuff we were assigned on Friday."

He used "maths" which she understood but could not bring herself to say. For her it was still the American word, "math."

"Not yet," she admitted. "We can go over the math assignment on Zoom tonight, and I can show you a couple of ways around some of tougher problems. And don't panic. We are only at the beginning of half-term break."

***

Simon Grasshwort rolled up the black plastic strap around the middle of his binoculars. He hitched up his green corduroy trousers. With the binoculars securely stowed into their leather case, he moved along at a leisurely pace away from the River Sheaf and then strolled the general direction of Melanie and Rafe. Changing course slightly, he steered within a yard or two of the pair sitting on the grass. Melanie thought she detected a furtive glance from the old gentleman in the direction of Rafe. When Simon was a safe distance away, she spoke with a touch of amusement in her voice.

"Who was that?"

"Ordinary park perv. This place is full of them."

Melanie was amused. "Ah, and they take an interest in certain sorts of young men?" They both laughed.

"Handsome ones, yes."

They both laughed again but this time there was an edge in Melanie's voice.

Chapter 3

Irie's Tribe

Fred was standing with Irie behind a crowd of onlookers at Millhouses pond when he suddenly spied a sleek, grey craft that he hadn't seen before, a model of a Japanese torpedo boat. Darting away from her, he quickly moved forward to get a better view. He wriggled in among the watchers. Some wearing COVID masks and some not.

Irie shouted, "Don't be an idiot, Fredrick. People don't have masks on." A few in the crowd turned to glower at her as if she, herself, were the idiot. Some were anti-maskers, but others just didn't like hearing young people making a commotion. Fred looked around. Stopped and thought. Then, abashed, momentarily ashamed, he roughly pushed his way out, in the process receiving a few unpleasant remarks. Irie wagged her finger at him in genuine rebuke. At first, he pleaded.

"Gimme a break, Irie . . . Merde!"

"'Merde'? Jeez Louise Freddie, boy. Must you practice your French when not in school?"

Fred quickly had enough of being rebuked and shifted from penitent sinner into serious bad boy mode. "I heard it on a TV show about French police. It was there along with 'putain.' Yes, putain and merde." These were words he had definitely not learned doing his French homework.

Irie, too, quickly shifted mood, but back towards sounding like friends-with him, again. She produced an angelic smile. "Are you saying those ugly words to annoy me? Or are you just trying to show to the world that you're a big, bad rebel?" He took her beatific smile as a concession. And she didn't really mind hearing "ugly" words every now and then.

"OK. I'll be good," he said and no doubt meant it.

"For a while," she said and no doubt doubted him.

"For a little while. A few days." He offered a compromise.

"More like a few hours." She was under no illusions.

The two walked away from the pond and to their bench in a pleasant cloud of relief. In addition, there were the warm breeze, the sunshine, and the people at the pond, who really weren't all that terrible. Only a very few didn't wear masks or wore them under their noses. The grumpiness of gormless grown-ups was left behind them. Irie liked that word, "gormless." She had no idea where it came from but it sounded like "clueless" and meant the same thing without being used as a title to a film.

Irie and Fred's bench was hidden away from the pond and back under a sessile oak tree. The tree had limbs like twisted arms ending in fingery branches. Oaks of that species, according to Fred, had been growing in the area since the ice sheets receded more than a 10,000 years ago. Other people didn't sit on the cold concrete bench much, so it was free to be used most of the time. It was covered at one end with orange lichen, but the two friends kept the other spotless. That's where they sat. This was their secret place. Private enough for any sort of conversation.

"Freddie, what's your tribe?" Irie began to probe into his life, as she sometimes did. "What's my what?" Fred might not have understood, but, then again, he might have been faking being thick, as Irie would have said. Thick as in thick in the head. Dense, blockhead.

"You know. People. Who are the people you come from?" Irie was genuinely interested and Fred decided to play along. He also knew that some revelation was coming, something that was intimate. Something that would be a tiny bit embarrassing, but he still wanted to hear it.

Fred: "Irie, you know where I come from. Arizona. Yuma. That's where my people are from. Where it's blazing hot right now. Hot here too, right now. But not as hot as . . . "

"No. Your people. Like I'm Windrush and Lascar." Irie was not quite sure if Fred knew about Windrush, though it was in the news sometimes. Black-and-white photos of a huge old steamship with black men and women standing at the railing. Negroes as they were called then. Men wearing ties. Men with hats on their heads because it was the 1950s. Women in print dresses. Also wearing hats of a different sort. Nobody in jeans. Lascar was another matter, something she would save for a later time on the same bench.

Fred did know about Windrush. That was the name of the ship. But he didn't have a clue about Lascar. He was often clueless or gormless, as boys his age sometimes were. Rather than get embarrassed as she continued to make revelations, he decided to tease, "And you're a princess. That's what you always say."

Her dark eyes became serious. She brushed off his teasing. "Yeah, that's what I sometimes say. But there is more to it. I've never told you this: "Tiny princess." That's what my name means. Irie: tiny princess in the language of Jamaica where my grandmother was born."

"Holy moly! That name is so cool. I always wondered about what it meant. Never knew. Afraid to ask. Mine's crap. 'Frederick.' And ancestry? I don't know all that much about my ancestry. If you go back far enough, Swedish maybe. But in America for a long time." Fred stood and looked at the sessile oak. "There may have been Confederate soldiers. You said "rebel," well that what they were, rebels. But not mythical heroes. The American Civil War, not the English one. And some of the descendants of those guys . . . Proud of a heritage of honor and service. Suffering and dying for a cause. I'll give them that. But slave owners, not a history to get puffed up about. A lost cause they said. They still say. I say, a lost cause and not a good one. Gone and best forgotten. Or, if not forgotten, then stored away like statues of racists now gathering dust in some stinking warehouse." That was quite a statement, thought Irie, who at first didn't know how to respond.

Irie: "We're a funny pair of people. Grandkids of inhabitants of another world, another time." She had decided to back away from emotional territory.

Fred sat and looked at the ground. "My heritage, for some of my relatives, is a cover for something else."

Irie refused to let him get sad. And she could not resist a joke that she saw in little bags of dog poo stacked in a pile beside a metal mesh trash can nearby. A "bin," as Irie would say. She motioned to the bin. Fred immediately brightened. "That's about it. The lost cause of the slave-owning South equals dog poo wrapped up in little bags." He suddenly dropped the topic of race as fast as she had. "Yesterday I saw a weird thing."

"Yeah?" Irie tilted her head to one side and gave Fred her winning, big-eyed look.

"Near dog poo tree," Fred replied with a sly smile.

"Tell on, oh man of weird stories."

And so Fred told her something that she might be able to guess more about than he did. "A boy went into the gennel near dog poo tree and disappeared. Older kid. Friends with my big sister. He goes to High Storrs School. Two years ahead of us, like she is."

The dog poo tree was a spot where walkers sometimes deposited their little bags rather than taking them to the bins. It was easy to do, even if you knew it was littering. Only you didn't think "littering." Someone else was sure to come along and clean it all up. If it was a crime against the environment, it was down at the bottom of the crime list. And they paid people to pick up after you.

Irie's interest was piqued. "Disappeared in dog-poo gennel. And the boy just vaporized right in the middle of the path? Like a fog going into the hedges on both sides of the gennel? Or maybe he melted like the witch in The Wizard of Oz. Did you look for a pool of water there on the ground?"

Fred was not happy, and he found her joking annoying. "Stop it." He growled. "This actually happened. Flashing light: Not funny. And it's not 'dog poo' gennel."

Irie: "Maybe the boy just went round the bend in the gennel." She liked to say "round" the bend. It sounded like "come round for tea."

Fred was definite: "There's no bend in the gennel. Irie, let's pay a visit to the corner shop. Go through Ireton Wood on the way. We can examine the mysterious gennel for secret passages." He was only half joking about "secret passages."

Irie feigned disbelief. "Given up on watching RC boats?"

Chapter 4

What Gennels Are

Fred pulled back the conifer branches in one wall of the tall, green gennel but could only see into someone's back garden. Lots of prickly branches. No secret passage. Now, it is a matter of fact that there are many sorts of gennels in Sheffield. Some long, some short, some narrow, some wide. This gennel was narrow with tall green hedges on both sides. It never saw daylight except at noon and stood just beyond the stone bridge of Totley Brook in Ireton Wood.

Fred: "You're right, Irie. There's a bend. No passage into another part of the galaxy. Merde!" He delivered his assessment with a shrug of the shoulders. Irie had no intention of gloating and was disappointed herself. A mystery would have livened things up a bit. "I'd rather he disappeared. That boy you saw . . . Do you really want to go to the corner shop right now? I'm drained. No energy. Sweaty weather."

"How about the brook under the stone bridge? It's down cool there." As Fred spoke, he looked into her face. She was a little moist across the forehead, and he resisted an urge to wipe the drops away with something. His hand, maybe. But no. Irie and Fred carefully worked their way from root foothold to root foothold down the slippery clay bank of the brook. When they reached the bottom, they plunked down on two large stones facing one another. Irie found herself ducking her head under the round arch of the bridge as she sat. There, under the arch, she spied an inscription carved into a large grit-stone block and mostly hidden by moss.

"Hey. Here's some writing," she said. Fred stood up, balancing himself precariously on two rocks that wobbled. He craned his neck so that he could see under the stone bridge.

Irie haltingly read aloud. "Speak. Say something of the Saxon . . . "

Fred took her hesitation as an opportunity to complete the sentence: "The next word is 'Warriors.'"

"Jeeze, Louise, Freddie boy. Will you let me finish?" Irie began again: "'Speak. Say something of the Saxon warriors. Chant for them who triumphed in the parlay at Dore.'" Irie was not about to let someone else finish a sentence for her.

Unfazed, Fred's enthusiasm bubbled up like Totley Brook itself. "The parlay at the village of Dore? King Ecgbert and his warriors triumphed at Dore. He was king of the Mercians and at Dore became ruler of the Northumbrians, too. That means pretty much the whole ball of wax. Gave his name to Ecgbert School."

Irie could not resist: "Freddie. You know a lot of stuff, even if it's useless. And 'ball of wax.'' Wherever did you get that one?"

Still unfazed, he looked her, smiled broadly and said, "Merde."

Irie continued: "And your parents shouldn't let you watch French police shows on TV. The dialogue. Swear words and utter filth." It might seem that she was trying to pop his happy balloon, but she wasn't. What she said had the opposite effect, as she knew it would. Fred was pleased that his special French words were finally getting the attention that they deserved, and both of them loved the phrase "utter filth." It seemed the sort of thing a prissy teacher would say quietly to herself about the way kids talk nowadays. Or maybe the teacher was "sir" and not "Miss." That's what you had to call them – sir for the men and Miss for the women. It was crazy, because a lot of the men were not really what you would think of as "sir." And the women? Mostly they were married and signed off as Ms.

Later that day in the evening when he was home, Fred removed a green paperback book from the middle shelf of an overstuffed bookcase. He sat on the floor of the hallway and examined its smudged cover, which announced Beowulf in facing pages of Anglo-Saxon language original on one side and Modern English translation on the other. There on the flyleaf was a note of ownership in what was sure to have been written with a fountain pen: EW Gustafson, Iowa 1985. And on the first left-hand page in Anglo-Saxon was the beginning of the poem itself:

"Hwaet we gardena." On the first right-hand page was the translation: "Lo! We the spear Danes." Fred had heard about Beowulf from the time when he was in pre-school. It was a movie that he had not seen. But mostly it was this: When your father's an English teacher, there are lots of books you hear about. Fred laid Beowulf on the floor beside him and plucked another book from the middle shelf. It was even-more dirty with fatherly smudges, but with a cloth cover: Henry Sweet's The Student's Dictionary of Anglo-Saxon.

He thought he might take Henry Sweet's Dictionary along with him the following day to show to Irie. Then he reconsidered. There was a pretty good chance that she would find it boring and find him boring for bringing it along. Decisions, decisions. What to do. He would decide in the morning.

Chapter 5

An Avocado-green Toilet

Fred walked along the sidewalk with a black backpack slung over his shoulder. It contained two borrowed books along with a package for Irie's friend, Lady Yerba. Fred had not asked his father for permission to take the smudged volumes, but it was abundantly clear that they were not going to be used by anyone else. Before long, he and Irie encountered the familiar red pillar mail box with the marking E II R, and Fred, as was his custom, spun around it. Irie was matter-of-fact, but at the same time she reminded him that they needed to stop on their way to Ireton Wood.

Irie: "We'll to drop in at Lady Yerba's. I love that house." She always praised things connected to Lady Yerba. "Funky. And the front garden. Beautifully overgrown. Gone back to nature."

Fred knew he had to endure the visit, but did give a shrug of agreement saying, "A predictable detour. You know, to tell the truth, her front yard gives me the creeps. Weeds, and more weeds. Knee-high Venus flytraps. Huge.

People eating. And the stuff you tell me to do to make Lady Yerba happy."

Irie: "She is a character. And, like me, she is a colourful person. A colourful person of colour."

Fred: "Your healthy skin shade and my pale face, what a combo, you and I. And. Lady Yerba is a colourful person of colour with a colourful toilet sitting in her front yard."

Irie: "Aren't we clever?"

Fred: "At least she isn't sitting on that junked toilet in her front yard." He was still American enough to insist on saying, "front yard" instead of "front garden," but he did push the matter just a little more than it needed to be pushed. He continued, "Lady Yerba should have someone cut the grass, trim back the blackberry brambles, and take the avocado-green toilet to the dump. Did people really have toilets that colour actually in their houses at some point in human history?"

Irie returned to Fred's comic exaggeration: "No man-eating or leg-grabbing plants in her front garden. You read too much sci-fi. And, of course, too much fantasy fiction. I'm sure the bin men will come round and cart off the toilet soon."

So was it a front "garden" or a front "yard"? Was it a weed patch or nature allowed to be free. Perhaps it was more like a barnyard than anything else, since two red and black hens scratched at open patches of dirt and pecked among the blades of grass. The avocado-green toilet was set alongside the driveway, and it was Lady Yerba's little cenote, a miniature sacred pool. Ironically, this woman, who Fred found so unnerving, could be counted as another American because she had come to Sheffield from North America. To be exact, she came from Yucatan in Mexico rather than further north – in the direction of Yuma. Yucatan was a place of many cenotes, pools sacred to the Maya. Indigenous people, those. Some were Christians and some trusted their shamans. Lady Yerba, herself, was seated in an old aluminium lawn chair with woven plastic seat and back. A second chair was empty and stood at COVID distance from her. Beside her was a bottle of hand disinfectant. Other chairs were folded and leaning against the house. Sacred pools or no sacred pools, Lady Yerba trusted in medical science.

"Buenos días, niños." Lady Yerba appeared to be somewhere in her late forties or early fifties, her face showing signs of her early life spent in a sunny part of the world.

Irie walked over to the toilet/cenote and gave it a tap with the toe of her Converse high-top. Her voice was full of sweet respect and awe for the woman, and at the same time her face betrayed a hint of fear. "We brought you the root that you wanted. It's in Fred's backpack. Wrapped in paper. How's everything?"

"Very good since you came along, hija." For her part, Lady Yerba had a kindly voice.

Irie issued a small, pleasant order to her friend, "Frederick, can you open the backpack and get out the root?"

Fred gave her a weary look and picked up the backpack. When he withdrew the root and unwrapped it, he was startled. This was no ordinary garden vegetable. It was purple with red highlights and was covered in places with orange hairs. "I didn't know you had that kind of stuff in there. It's my backpack. Holy moley. You should let me know what sort of magic plants you're making me carry. That one definitely looks dangerous."

Though she wasn't, Irie made a point of sounding offended: "It's our backpack, really, and no need for each of us to have one when we can share toting it about."

Hoping to break into the tense atmosphere that had been developing, Fred said with his twisty smile, "Have I used up my quota filthy French words for the day? Or can I comment?"

Rather than be shocked by what Fred had just said, Lady Yerba was amused and even pleased. Irie answered his question with a long-suffering look in her eyes: "You have, indeed, gone over your quota, young man. I've had to pardon your French far too often in the last few days."

Lady Yerba's face showed that she continued to enjoy the low-level tension between the two friends. She saw, or thought she saw something about the two of them that they did see themselves. Her voice was kindly, even sentimental. It was as if she were remembering about when she was a girl back in Merida. Lady Yerba: "Irie, you are so polite and you remember to do as you have promised."

Fred: "Can we go now?" He, already impatient, was drifting into the bad-boy version of himself.

Irie countered his lack of social graces: "Jeez Louise. Don't be an oaf, Freddie."

For whatever reason, Lady Yerba knew where the two would be going next. "I won't keep you two young people from this beautiful day, except to ask after my friends the Spanish bluebells in Ireton Wood." Irie, herself, was now becoming uncomfortable and was ready to move along. A little too much "happy" can be wearing."

Not trying to be deflating, but just giving a report, Irie said, "Mostly gone now. Pretty blue flowers in Ireton Wood gone to seed. Sorry to say."

"Qué lástima. Well, run along the pair of you. You have much to do today."

How did she know how much they needed to do? Actually, they didn't think they had anything to do. Irie and Fred started down the driveway back to the street. Irie stopped, took Fred by the shirt, and turned him around. She pointed him back up the drive. Irie: "Do I have to?" Fred moaned as skulked his way back up the driveway to give the cenote/toilet a small tap with his Converse. This is what Irie had told him would make Lady Yerba happy, and it did. And, having completed his assigned task, he stopped moaning. And Irie thought to herself: "I wish he weren't always a mardy bum." But he noticed, as the tip of his toe touched the green porcelain, just a slight tingle, a tingle similar to the one he experienced when he touched the rune on the lychgate.

The two friends made their way down to the city street, and as they walked along, the red post of a mailbox came into view. Irie: "Thanks for that, Freddie." She was genuinely pleased. "Thanks for giving that sociable tap on the cenote. It means a lot to her. She's old and God knows what sort of stuff she believes in. Probably Shamans and that kind of thing. Spiritual men of the Maya. You see it as a toilet, but it's her little, baby cenote. They have big ones in Yucatan. Mexico. Limestone sink holes. That's where she comes from, Mexico."

Fred: "Yucatan? Mexico? Cool. And I thought sink holes were only in Florida. Swallowers of houses." Then he added an unwelcome afterthought. "But you and Lady Yerba are both creepy. Not just her."

Irie was for a moment shocked, offended. But the sudden reaction wore off and she took his remark as a complement. She liked the idea of being a little mysterious, though she knew that she, herself, was the complete opposite of creepy. She simply replied with complete confidence, "You don't mean that, Freddie boy."

Chapter 6

Mathematics Homework

It was the day after Rafe and Melanie were sitting on the lawn at Millhouses Park, the day after the two joked about the elderly Simon Grasshwort of the green corduroys and the muddy shoes. But today was today and Rafe, who was now alone, briskly walked to the middle of the stone bridge in Ireton Wood, where he abruptly stopped. This was the stone bridge under which Irie and Fred had sheltered from the heat the day before and where they found the writing about the Anglo-Saxons at the village of Dore. Rafe mumbled something to himself in a strange rhythm, and then he walked over towards the gennel. Into the gennel he went, and there was no mistaking it. Rafe slowly drifted out of focus and disappeared right at the bend in the wall of the conifer hedge.

Rafe's disappearance was only temporary, however, as he showed up that evening for an appointment with Melanie at a Zoom homework session, a meeting that included only the two of them. On the wall behind Melanie and appearing on Rafe's screen was a Diego Rivera poster of a Mexican girl with a large bunch of calla lilies. Behind

Rafe was a framed poster of the racing driver Lewis Hamilton standing beside a Mercedes belonging his formula-one team. Rafe did not mince words or beat around the bush: "OK, numbers girl. How do I get answers for the homework?"

She could feel him pushing her and did not want to do his homework for him. She knew at the same time that he was at her mercy, a fact which she enjoyed. Her voice was that of a very kindly math teacher when Melanie said, "So if 1x equals 0.777 where the sevens keep on going forever, then solve for x." He was not happy with her mathematical puzzle, which he understood as a stupid waste of time. Her question was not relevant to the homework assigned, but he did definitely want her help.

Therefore, he decided to humour her and suppressed a snarl as he played along, "Not possible. You can't know a number that goes on forever. No way to solve for x." He paused and tossed the problem back at her, "Let's not play games tonight. Or if we are doing games right now, then I give up. You win."

Melanie was not about to let him off the hook that easily: "Show Melanie what an intelligent boy you are. Use your devious wiles. Or, failing that, use your mathematical imagination." Melanie had a cruel streak, which Rafe sometimes brought out, though he was just thick-skinned enough to not be offended when she talked down to him. And right now that is how she was talking. Indeed, she was doing an excellent imitation of a different sort of woman math teacher, one that was not so kindly. If

Rafe had a little more wit about him, he might have sarcastically called her "Miss Gustafson."

What he said instead was, "Don't be a tease, Mel."

And, of course, Melanie was teasing him in more than one way. She was trying to tease out some sort of mathematical understanding in his brain, and she was teasing him as girls tease boys they like. So, Melanie went on teasing: "If you are going to go chasing after the female children of royals at St Bearnard's Uni in Scotland, you'll need to understand an equation or two. You'll need to get some A's on your A-level math exams. History exams, too. Otherwise you will go to a university that you don't want."

Rafe had his heart set on finishing high school in Sheffield and becoming a handsome, eligible undergraduate male in Scotland. Melanie was right about the kids at the University of St Bearnard. It did attract wealthy and spoiled children whose parents were lord and lady something. Occasionally there was a really big fish among this privileged bunch – a child descended from kings and queens. Maybe a child who was weird and on some sort of spectrum, but still a descendent from rulers and "the right sort of people."

Melanie knew she was being a little unfair. St Beanie's was an academically good place "to go to college," as she would have said if she'd stayed with her brother in Yuma. There, even going to Flagstaff to attend Northern Arizona University was "college." College out of the Sonoran Desert and into the snowy Ponderosa pines. Truth to tell, secretly she would not mind accepting an offer from

Beanie's herself. She and Rafe were both exploring possibilities in the college market, sharing information and keeping little bits from one another. Each would be somewhere not in Sheffield come this time next year. Which is not to say that Melanie would follow Rafe anywhere, or so she told herself. She turned out to be right about this, but only after some twists and turns that neither expected.

Rafe was losing patience with Melanie the math boffin and he knew how to set her off. "What's wrong with good-looking, nicely turned out girls who are blood kin of royals? Saint Beanie is at the top of the ratings for Scottish history. Let's be truthful about the situation It's as easy to marry one of those girls as it is to . . ." He then switched gears before she could say anything, "I told you, Mel. It can't be solved for x. When are we going to get down to real work and stop mucking about."

If Melanie was triggered by the reference to the posho girls as marriage material, she did a good job of not letting on, and her response to Rafe was delivered in a cheerful tone: "Nicely turned out really means wearing expensive clothes bought by mommy at Harrod's in London." At the same time, she enjoyed thinking to herself, "Oh yes it can be solved. It's not all that difficult to find the value of for x if you think about it and you were not such a dumb ass."

Quite suddenly and for no apparent reason, the two of them stopped poking at one another verbally and set about doing their mathematics homework together. Rafe, for his part, was not nearly as bad with numbers one might have thought from listening to him, but he did like to have his homework checked over by an expert before he nonchalantly dropped it on the teacher's desk. While the two of them launched their attacks, they were also careful to not finish certain nasty sentences and to say under their breaths rather than speak out loud certain thoughts. Yet, they knew what was in the sentence that was not completed and what was said under the breath.

And so Melanie mumbled to herself: "As easy to marry into a royal family as to marry to a girl from some desert town in the American Southwest? Home of the Yuma High School Criminals." And she liked the smell of the creosote bush after a rain or the feel of the air in Flagstaff when it was 40 degrees Celsius in Yuma.

Chapter 7

The Girl in White

On the same day and at the time that Rafe faded away in the tall, green gennel, Irie and Fred were at their favourite bench at Millhouses Park, the bench overlooked by the twisty-fingered sessile oak. Irie reached down and lifted Fred's backpack onto her lap. She took out the smudged copy of Beowulf with the green cover and the facing page versions in Anglo-Saxon and Modern English.

"I could never read this stuff." Irie looked amused: "It may be Old English but I will never be old enough to read it. And isn't it confusing to say 'Anglo-Saxon' and 'Old English' and mean the same thing?" Fred did not attempt to respond to her barrage of remarks, but that was OK with her. She proceeded to rummage around in his backpack for a second time and came up with Henry Sweet's Anglo-Saxon Dictionary.

"That's a classic," observed Fred. "Sweet's dictionary has been around for more than a hundred years and it still works just fine."

Irie could not resist the opportunity to have a joke at the expense of the man who lived a hundred years ago.

"Did someone say 'sweet'? Time to head to the corner shop for a Fredo. A nice, very little, very chocolate, and very sweet froggie." Irie knew all about Fred's weakness for inexpensive chocolate frogs called Fredos. The two of them stood, and Fred slung the backpack over one shoulder. They trudged away towards the Spar, their favourite convenience store. That would take them through Ireton Wood and, if they went the short way, through a stand of holly bushes and into the gennel where Rafe had disappeared.

Ireton Wood was full of walkers that day. People with dogs and people just out for a stroll. A woman wearing a bright yellow hi-vis jacket and riding a large bay horse came up from behind on what was both a bridal path and a walking trail. She passed them and trotted out of the wood into a city street on which there were a few cars. Fred looked a little puzzled and said, "That woman. It says POLITE on the back of her hi-vis jacket. But the jacket looks like a POLICE jacket, the sort of thing they wear when there are mounted police for a Sheffield United football match at Bramall Lane." Then he started thinking: "But I'm beginning to I understand."

Irie broke in for just a second: "Sussed it out, have we?" She paused and looked happy.

Fred, too, was pleased, that she let him continue without going on to provide the answer. Fred: "Some cars roar past people on horses, but nobody does that when they think it's the police."

"A good lie," said Irie. "A lie to save lives."

"More like a good misdirection," said Fred. "Not quite a lie."

"I'll stick with lie," said Irie, and they trudged on among the bluebells that Lady Yerba so loved, the bells of the flowers now replaced with green seeds the size of peas. Although it wasn't allowed, Irie and Fred regularly took the shortcut off the path. They were about to emerge from a stickery holly bush, but they stopped as if they both knew separately – but for the same hidden reason – that they shouldn't be seen.

What had made them stop was the sight of Mr Grasshwort, the man of the green corduroys and the muddy shoes, emerging from the gennel, but he didn't just come walking out in an ordinary way. It was as if he were an image that was beginning to slide into focus in a cellphone camera. After that the man of the muddy shoes had become a human being and not a hologram. He left the bridge and furtively approached the dog poo tree, where several little baggies of poo had been placed at the base of the trunk. There he deposited a bag of his own. Irie and Fred couldn't see from so far away in the holly bush, but in fact the bag was not tied in in the usual way in a knot. Instead, it had a red twisty to keep it closed. When he twisted the twisty, they could see that. With this task accomplished Mr Grasshwort casually walked away by the path that Irie and Fred should have been using.

The two friends gave one another puzzled looks as they emerged from the narrow space between two stickery holly bushes. Neither was quite ready to discuss the matter of the old man. As if nothing had happened, Irie took the backpack from Fred and reached down inside. She extracted Henry Sweet's The Student's Dictionary of Anglo-Saxon and began to page through it. Fred did not quite fathom what was going on with the book and, slightly irritated, said, "I thought we were going to the corner shop. Sweets. Chocolate. A frog. Remember?" Irie walked towards the stone bridge, continuing to turn the pages. She left the backpack on the ground. Fred, who was none too happy, picked it up and followed her.

As she got to the centre of the bridge she said, almost to herself but in a way that Fred could easily hear, "There's got to be something in this book that will explain the inscription." She was, of course, referring to the words written in the stone that they had found the day before. She stood there flipping the pages, getting nowhere, or at least that is what was Fred's view.

He reached for the book saying, "Give it me."

But she pulled it back towards herself. Then, a few seconds later, she handed it across to him saying, "Give it me? OK, sure. But don't make fun of my accent."

Fred seemed to be deep into the book but he said, almost as if to nobody: "It's not your accent, it's your grammar." The truth is that Fred was not making fun of Irie by saying "Give it me." It is just that he had let the language of Sheffield creep into his speech. Had he stayed in Yuma, he would have said "Give it to me."

And Irie? She actually knew and thought it was fun that he was falling into Sheffield dialect. Nonetheless Irie said, "You should never cross a South Yorkshire woman. You're not in Yuma now. And you have got to stop wearing that tee. Does your mother ever wash it?"

Fred looked up, suppressed a giggle, and handed her Mr Sweet's grammar without comment. She took it and began to scan for words connected to Ecgbert's warriors and the village of Dore. Words like, "triumph" and "spears." Fred was about to walk to the gennel to give it another look, when he saw a girl out of the corner of his eye. She was wearing white shorts and a billowy white cotton top. Her top like was like the one worn by pirates in the TV show Poldark. The girl's skin was pale, as was her hair, which was tied with a blue Alice band. He turned to get a better look and she gave him a little wave before disappearing into the holly. She had, in fact, been standing precisely where he and Irie had stood when they saw Mr Grasshwort come out of the gennel.

Somehow Fred was unnerved and he felt a little faint. Looking around for a place to sit down, he found a large rock a little distance away from the stone bridge and towards the gennel. There sat to collect his thoughts – or maybe regain his composure. His heart slowed and he began to catch his breath.

"What are you doing over there?" Irie called out when she saw that he had left her side. "Are you OK? You look a bit pekid, like you've just seen the ghost of Julius Caesar." They had been reading Shakespeare's *Julius Caesar* in English, and the remark was meant as a joke. However, Irie, seeing him looking not-so-good, suddenly began to feel not-so-good herself. As Fred regained his composure, both felt better. He stood and walked back to her, but he did not mention the girl in white. He didn't have many secrets from Irie, and this was one of the few. Most strange of all, he wasn't sure why he didn't just automatically tell Irie about this girl. The white shorts. The white cotton top. The TV pirate show. Into the bargain, was the fact that his parents had watched a TV series called The Woman in White, something just a touch spooky. That connection might have given him material for joke of some sort, but he kept quiet.

Irie suspected that something was going on with her friend, and from the corner of her eye she had just barely seen a person disappear behind the holly bush. Rather than let herself become freaked out, she decided to get the two of them moving, and so she spoke, "Freddie, you know what we could do? I could stand at the holly bush and film you on my mobile while you walk into the gennel. That old dude with the muddy shoes. He seemed to materialize like an Enterprise crew member beamed down by Scotty. But maybe it was just sunlight light coming in spots through little places in the gennel hedge. So you stand over there. Walk around, and I'll film you. Then we can both look at the result."

"A shoot for a cell-phone camera movie? Enter a film festival." Fred was back to being himself. And, 'dude' did you really say 'dude.' You always complain that word is used too much by Americans."

Irie ignored the remark about her drift into American dialect. She was both embarrassed and pleased to be caught in the act. Maybe she was starting to talk like Yuma and not Sheffield. Returning to the topic of the cell-phone movie, she slyly promised him, "I'll make you a star. But no funny walks. This is not Monty Python." The two of them had seen a few YouTube clips of the Pythons.

And when Fred said, "And don't put it on Insta without my permission," it might have been more an invitation than anything else. Irie tilted her head a little to one side and opened her eyes wide like a silent-movie love interest. Irie said in deadpan tone: "Would I?"

That night, Irie sat at her desk intent on what she was seeing on her laptop. She picked up her mobile phone and called Fred. Not bothering with any small talk, she launched into her reason for calling: "You know how we couldn't really see anything unusual on my mobile after we filmed at the gennel? Well, I looked at the video clip on my lap-top screen, and the picture of you did turn a fuzzy as you got to the bend in the gennel. Only a little. We need to go back there tomorrow. Or maybe not. This is all getting pretty silly. Like a TV series. We shouldn't make it into a big deal that it isn't." She was silent for a time, listening while he replied. Then, she used the South Yorkshire "ta" for "good-bye," not her usual practice with Fred. But she did say it when she was especially happy or a little worried. Or both at the same time.

Chapter 8

Into the Gennel

Early the next morning, there was speckled shade at the gennel. Sunlight shone through the conifer hedge on its east side and splashed in spots on the ground. The stone bridge was showing the remains of morning dew when Rafe crossed to its centre. He said a single word several times in a loud whisper, loud enough to be heard if anyone had been there, though outside of a few runners and the odd walker not many ever were ever around at this time of day. There was a rhythm in the way Rafe delivered what he said, and he betrayed a certain nervous jerkiness as he stood. When he spoke, he looked around to see if there were any listeners, which there were not. Then, seeing that the coast, was clear, he briskly walked into the gennel. There was no mistaking it now, he gradually faded from view as he came to the bend. Then he disappeared completely.

If Irie and Fred had arrived a few minutes earlier, they would have been witness to the whole business of the older boy, the kid from year 13 at High Storrs School, disappearing in the dappled shade of the deep green gennel.

As it was, the two emerged from the holly bushes and proceeded to the middle of the stone bridge being none the wiser. Irie would have kept going, but Fred stopped and looked down into the water, which was quite low and hardly running. Fred was in a pensive mood. He wasn't unhappy but he was pretty far away from his usual outgoing, optimistic self. Irie thought about pulling him by his shirt towards the gennel and from there steering him to the Spar convenience store with its abundant chocolate frogs. She often did this sort of thing by tugging on his sleeve, but she was, herself, in a bad mood, and she teased Fred in a tone of voice that wasn't very nice. Her mother would sometimes say that "You're not being very nice." What popped out of Irie's mouth was, "I thought you wanted to go to the shops today, Freddie boy. You were keen to buy a chocolate frog. Going to the Spar to buy 'something.' Something in a dead language." She knew that he would not like the phrase "dead language."

The day before Irie had found the word "hwathwegu" in Henry Sweet's dictionary of Anglo-Saxon. She had been randomly looking at entries and came across this one, which means quite literally, "something." Irie coyly asked Fred if he wanted her to find something in the dictionary, and he agreed, not knowing that she was setting him up for a joke. Fred was completely unimpressed when Irie hit him with the punch line: "Then here it is. Hwaethwegu.

'Something' in Anglo-Saxon, if you want to believe Henry Sweet – 'something' is 'hwathwegu.'"

Fred had replied with bored sarcasm that, "Nobody likes a smart ass."

So what was causing the difficulty between the two of them on this, the day after the joke that failed? They were both separately mulling over their discussion of the disturbing video from the night before. And Fred also had the girl in white floating somewhere in the back of his head. Deep in the recesses of his mind knew his feeling of self-yucchiness was partly tied to the video and partly to the girl with the billowy, white cotton top. The white shorts and the white cotton top. The whole business of female pirates. Consciously he was just himself, clueless as ever. Gormless as a guy can be.

"Don't be an EMO," said Irie, a remark that did not ease the tension of the situation.

Fred responded with the single word "hwathwegu," which he chanted at her rhythmically three times acting as if he were an evil sorcerer. He raised his arms as if to fly and his chant was loud. HWATHWEGU. HWATHWEGU. HWATHWEGU.

She tried to cool off the situation. "Oh, all right, let's go to the Spar and get that Fredo you want so much. I can understand. I'd like a bit of chocolate myself. AND, to tell the truth, you're not an EMO. You're my bestest, best friend. But no more chanting. It feels spooky and you'll disturb the herons in the bird sanctuary. They'll never breed again because of you." There were signs posted in

Ireton Wood warning against the effects of too much noise on the breeding patterns of the herons. The joke at the end of what she said worked its magic.

For the moment, they were both silently happy, and then Fred said, "To the Spar for a Fredo? I'll do that in a New York minute. A Yuma minute, which is slower but gets the job done more thoroughly. And thanks. I think that video was getting me freaked out. There's warm sun on the other side of the gennel and I am ready for it. Time to de-freak." Irie was relieved that they were back on good terms. She, too, wanted to de-freak.

And so the two friends, back to being friends again, strolled into the high, green gennel. As they rounded the bend, they seemed to dissolve like an image in a cell-phone camera going out of focus. Then they were gone.

***

It was absolutely pitch black in the place they were after they vanished from the gennel. The air had a musty smell like an attic that had been closed for a hundred years or like a shoe box of letters that had only been opened after being lost long since. "Fred, are you there?" Irie spoke evenly. Her voice was more calm than was usual for her, a change that happened when she was in a tight situation.

Fred more clearly showed that he was unnerved by the total darkness and even slightly frightened. "Irie, what happened? I can't see anything." Irie was a person who did not mind giving orders, especially to certain, selected boys her own age and said, "I bet we're under it. The gennel. Underground. Get your mobile out of our backpack and turn on the torch. I want to see where we are."

Fred was put off by her barking orders. He responded, "Turn on YOUR OWN cell phone flashlight. And I want to see where we are, too." He often resisted when he thought he was being given tasks to do and when she was being "me, me, me." This silly refusal to do as she requested at least got his mind off of his present situation. It caused him to forget about the darkness and the musty odour for a moment or two.

Irie: "Mine's in your backpack, too." She had a point there and was wise enough to admit that the backpack was his. He had been carrying it over one shoulder when the two visually wobbled out of sight at the bend. He should be able to get both the phones with ease. Instead, a sudden terror got the best of him.

Fred: "I hate this place. It's dark and it stinks. I think something died in here. An animal." Fred was losing control. "Maybe a person died in here. He could be rotting at our feet. Don't move or you might slip in the muck from the corpse."

This time Irie joked him out of his panic by using Sheffield slang: "Don't be a mardi bum. Get a grip!" Then she came up with the solution: "Oh, I can feel the backpack with my feet. You dropped it on the floor. Hang on." Without thinking about it, Fred had set down the backpack where they were standing. And Fred was indeed beginning to get a grip. He could feel with his fingers that there were walls. The walls were cold and damp, made of some sort of soft brick, he guessed. He, too, thought that they were underground, and he wanted to have a look around. That said, he didn't like being called a "mardi bum" even when she used an affectionate tone. He knew the American English equivalent worked out to "sorry ass."

Sometimes being sorry ass was cool, and that is the way she said "mardi bum." Fortunately for the both of them and after some rummaging around in the backpack, Irie found a device that would do the job. That is, she used her mobile phone (as she would have said) or her cell phone (as he would have said) to fill with light the long, narrow passageway in which they stood. Fred had been right. The walls were made of brick and they sloped in straight lines towards the top, which was covered by a flat ceiling. He was in total awe.

In a state of serene calm, he began to consider the passageway as a piece of architecture. "This is absolutely freaky. These walls form a long corbelled arch. We are time transported to the Middle Ages. It could be the period of the Plantagenet kings. This might have been a tunnel for bringing water to the city of Sheffield, but the pipes that would be on the floor are long-since gone. And then, the big question. The really massive question. Why are we here? It's gotta be connected to what we were doing at Lady Yerba's house. We're here because we tapped the green toilet with our toes. That toilet has powers. Toilet, pipes, plumbing. So here we are. We'll figure a way out. We'll find way back to the present. Back to 2020. Do you think she's a witch. Bruja, isn't that the word for her in Spanish? Lady Yerba? Did you know that already?"

Irie was hugely relieved that Fred was de-freaked and chattering away like a magpie, but she was also annoyed by his suggestion that Lady Yerba was behind what had happened to them. And Lady Yerba was not a bruja. Irie: "Jeez Louise, Fred. That tiny green cenote already has protected us. At the lychgate. My mum and little brother couldn't see us. That's why I always have you give the cenote a gentle tap o' the toe. Protection. Please don't get paranoid. Lady Yerba is on our side in this."

Fred didn't quite like her tone of voice and was by no means ready to see Lady Yerba as their saviour. Fred decided to match her joke with one of his own. Fred: "On our side in this? Who's on the other side? Voldemort?"

Chapter 9

The Hob and the Hobgoblin

Irie had a good laugh. "Lord Voldemort? You gotta be kidding." For his part, Fred was on a roll: "These bricks aren't like what you'd find today. They're way old. Thin red bricks like the Romans made. And toilet bowl lady. If she isn't a witch then she's definitely a weirdo. How did we get here, oh woman of much wisdom?" His tag for her, "woman of much wisdom" had a mixed tone. It was a little hostile but also imploring. Maybe she did know something he didn't. Except, of course, about Roman building materials.

Irie: "It was your screeching that horrible Anglo-Saxon word those three times. That got us in here, into this long, narrow dungeon. Lord knows what will get us out. But we will get out and have stories to tell our grandchildren." They chuckled together as they both liked this line. When they had finished lifting each other's spirits, they examined the passage of soft, most red brick. At one end, right next to them was a wall of white limestone that had gone a little black with mold in places. The other end was not in sight. In its place, a long straight line of brick wall and stone floor was lost in the darkness. "Let's get going," she said – said rather than ordered. That was his view of what to do next as well as hers, and the two friends went in the only direction they could go.

Irie and Fred carefully made their way in single file along the narrow passageway in silence, though they could hear one another breathing and they could feel the flapping footfalls of their Converse tennies. Or was it trainers, as the people in Sheffield said? No matter which. Theirs was breathing that would have echoed, except that the brick was so soft and absorbent. The footfalls had a slight splash to them, for the damp stone floor had shallow puddles they could barely see. That breathing and those footfalls reassured the both of them. Each knew, "I am alive. I'm moving. I'm not alone. Thank god, I'm not alone."

And then a blue-white light appeared up ahead. As Irie and Fred continued on, they could see that it was coming from an opening on the right side of the brick wall. When they got closer, it became clear that the opening was a doorway with a pinewood frame. But there was no door and no hinges in the frame. Fred was in the lead and looked back at Irie. She gave him a little wobbly smile as if to say, "Go ahead and give it a look. It'll be OK."

Edging up to the doorway, Fred looked in, keeping his body back from view. And there in a large limestone cavern was someone standing in the LED light. Dozens of tiny LED spots in an artificial ceiling shown down on that small someone. It was someone whose face might have been seen if that someone had not had his back to Fred – a small man standing on a stool in front of a hob, stirring a large cast-iron pot. He was wearing a red shirt with a buff vest and blue jeans. A leather vest like a European peasant. From the waist up he seemed to be dressed from a long-ago era, a time when men and women harvested wheat with sickles and then fell asleep in the fields after lunch – a jug of wine by them on the stubbly ground. From the waist down, however, the little man might have been a hipster, for he was wearing black skinny jeans and footwear from Russell and Bromley in London. He had a long pointy chin like a witch. But no wart and rather a carefully trimmed hipster goatee. He was hipster top and bottom but peasant in the middle.

The little man continued stirring and without turning to look, said to Fred, "Come on in. You're late."

Fred pulled his head back and asked Irie in a whisper, "Did you hear that?"

She had indeed heard and gave him a little push so that he knew. She then asked the inevitable string of questions. Irie: "Who was it? Sounded like a 'he.' What does he look like? What do we do next?" Fred was a little put off by her barrage of questions. And "What do we do next?" She would have a few suggestions, herself.

Fred: "Yes, I saw him. It's a 'he.' He didn't even turn around. AND. He knew we were coming. And that's odd. I didn't know we were coming." Irie of course had done some figuring and her question about "What do we do next?" was merely a prelude to her outlining a plan that she already had hatched.

"What we do," said Irie, with a sense of complete sureness, is to march in there as casual and as cool as if we were taking a walk along the River Sheaf on a pleasant Sunday afternoon. Birds chirping. Dogs pulling at leashes.

Fred put the finishing touches on her plan. "Cool as a couple of cucumbers. That's us." And that is what they did. They sauntered into Hobgoblin's kitchen as if they were in the lobby of a cinema at the Meadow Hall mall. Meadow Hell, as Irie's mom would have said. And the connection would not have been a bad one because for all the two friends knew they were marching into hell, Irie thinking all time but not saying: "I wonder if Fred's wearing his tee shirt – Yuma High School Criminals – will help or hurt the situation in which we found ourselves?" And then she thought: "Probably will help."

What they saw instead of Hades or the Infernal Regions was a completely modern and fully equipped kitchen. The cooktop, or hob where Hobgoblin stood on his chair, worked by electrical induction. It was completely up to date and not an artefact of ten years ago, much less Medieval England. That said, the choice of cooktop/hob did not involve an easy decision for Hobgoblin as he worked out with the designers what sort of kitchen to have. He liked the great, huge gas hobs that high-end restaurants always have, but the cave in which he lived was not plumbed for natural gas and it did have a good connection to mains electricity, a connection so installed that the electric company was none the wiser. When Irie and Fred had made their way to what they took to be a safe distance from him, Hobgoblin turned and said, "Don't just stand there. Get a couple of bowls from the cupboard there over next to the fridge." The fridge was large and had a bright stainless-steel sheen. Unlike older, small fridges, this one was American. And did that mean it was made in America? No, it was made in Germany, for, as it turns out, Germans enjoy making American fridges. And Hobgoblin, he must have polished it when he wasn't cooking. Or maybe he had someone to do that for him. No, he did it himself.

They were startled by Hobgoblin's words but said nothing and did as they were told. When they had the beechwood bowls in their hands, they stood side by side and waited for further instructions. Hobgoblin spoke, "Don't you have brains enough to come here without being told to do so? Are ye unspeakably daft or do ye have sense enough to get a ladle or two of the best gungoi west of the River Sheaf?" He meant, of course, the river where Elaine Grasshwort had once gathered wild garlic, the river that ran by Millhouses Park.

Now the fact was that Fred was ravenously hungry and the odours that drifted towards him and Irie were seductively inviting. So, without further prompting, Fred strolled forward to receive his portion. Irie was not exactly pleased to be left standing there alone. She did not hold with the rule that "girls go first," but she did expect her friend to at least look at her before he bolted in the direction of scoff.

Indeed, before Irie could walk to the little man and his ladle, Fred was sitting with a full bowl at a long oak table marked with many years of use. That table now was edged in a fashionable aluminium band of ammonite blue and topped with strong safety glass. Fred eagerly lit into the bowl using an heirloom "made in Sheffield" spoon that he found set atop a white cloth napkin on the table. In the centre of the table was a large, deep wooden bowl (also beech) that contained fresh focaccia bread. Pausing from spooning up the gungoi, Fred reached for a piece of the focaccia and broke it in half. He scooped a wedge of butter from a crockery dish made by a talented local potter and sold at a pricy boutique. Sold at such a boutique or maybe borrowed by a goblin in the middle of the night. Hobgoblin was something of a playful spirit, and in this was like Puck in *Midsummer Night's Dream*. And he had exquisite taste in stoneware. As for the electric company, it could afford to supply his kitchen as an act of public service.

Irie could have murdered Fred as she watched all of this. And Fred would have richly deserved such a quietus. "Quietus" was a word Irie had picked up when they read *Hamlet* at High Storrs School back in January, and now was the time to let the word leap into her thoughts. But rather than continue to enjoy the sweet fantasy of a violent, Shakespearian end for her friend, she acceded to the fate of all (or maybe "many") teenage girls who find themselves in the company of hungry teenage boys. She decided to stoically endure Fred's lack of social graces and was soon sitting across from him at the table with her own beechwood bowl of gungoi. She, too, had a healthy appetite, but she wondered if it was wise to be eating in such strange circumstances. What if this little man was not a nice guy? What if he was the opposite of nice? Her mother's words echoed in her mind. And, still, she had the feeling that she was not going to be harmed by eating. Quite the reverse. She knew deep somewhere inside that the food would help her later in the day when she was running out of steam. And at the same time, she knew that this fellow, this tiny man was both a good 'un and a person who was not entirety helpful every single time. He was the sort of creature that might withhold information for what he thought were perfectly good reasons. Not that they were.

"This is pretty tasty, actually," said Fred as he wiped the bottom of his wooden bowl with a chunk of focaccia bread. Fred was happy and relaxed, recovering from the shock of finding himself at a dead end in a corbelled arch passageway.

Irie chimed in with a likewise favourable assessment, "Yes, Freddy boy. Bang on target. You are so right. I just love, love carrot and coriander soup. It is definitely my favourite."

Hobgoblin roared at the both of them, "You dare to sit in judgment of my gungoi, as if it was ordinary carrot and coriander! Who do you think you are? The Fairy Queen, mayhap?"

The two sat silent for what seemed an eternity. Then Irie spoke, "My apologies, Mr..."

The Hobgoblin continued in a nearly normal voice, though one in which there was plenty of sarcasm, "No apologies. I can't stand apologies. Won't abide 'em. And, do you expect me to tell you my name before you have spoken yours – in my kitchen? In MY kitchen? In front of MY hob?"

"Don't tell him, Irie." As Fred issued his warning, he suddenly realized that he had given away Irie's name. He went funny in the face for an instant which then shifted back to its normal self when Irie said reassuringly, "It's OK, Fred. Nobody who is evil could make carrot and coriander soup like this. It's definitely not from Tesco's." She meant the supermarket where her mother shopped. It was a nice place, nice enough to be boring.

Hobgoblin boiled over in rage once again, though this time in a controlled sort of way. "If either of you says Tesco again in this kitchen, I will turn you both into sparrows."

It was Fred and not Irie who understood the social situation this time and spoke appropriately. That was another one of Irie's mother's words, "appropriately," a word that set her teeth on edge. Fred, the hero of the moment, simply said, "There is not very much room in these wooden bowls. I didn't get enough. Can I have some more?"

Chapter 10

Polite Conversation in the Kitchen

Hobgoblin was about as pleased as a hobgoblin could be by Fred's request for another bowl of gungoi. He hopped down from his perch on the stool at the hob, scampered to the two friends' table, and picked up Fred's bowl. He scooted back to his stool, hopped up, filled the bowl, hopped down, and returned to plunk the brimming bowl in front of a delighted Fred. And that wasn't all. Hobgoblin then set two slices of bitter orange tart on wooden plates. These he took to the two friends with ceremony and pomp. He even made a low bow with his right arm spread out wide in the manner of a courtier of the time of Shakespeare. Hobgoblin was happy, but he did not forget to correct the grammar of Fred, who, of course, liked correcting others' grammar, himself.

Hobgoblin: "'May I.' Not 'can I.' And there's a good lad. . . But we need to talk. There is much work to be done. When we have spoken, there will be some bitter chocolate to drink. Good chocolate from Mexico. Chocolate made with boiling water. Not so sweet. Too much sugar is not so good for anyone. The chocolate goes well with the bitter orange tart." Irie and Fred were charmed. Here was a goblin who talked gruffly like someone's aged grandfather and who fed them like a sought-after chef who worked at a trendy restaurant on Ecclesall Road. The moment of serenity did not last.

There was the sound of heavy stumbling in the corbelled-arch passageway, words in a male voice cursing. Perhaps a vile lout caught had his foot on an uneven spot in the floor. That person was Rafe, who stopped and stood at the entry to Hobgoblin's kitchen. Rafe, who was not really a lout, held in his hand a tiny LED flashlight. He put down his backpack, unzipped it, and took out a dog poo bag. That bag was secured with a red twisty. He did not look into the kitchen for the simple reason that he did not know it was there.

He could be seen by Irie, Fred, and Hobgoblin, but could not see them in return. Where there had been a pinewood doorway (without a door to open and close) for Irie and Fred, there was just more moist, soft Roman brick in front of Rafe. Rafe opened the bag, sniffed and then returned it to the backpack. Pleased that he had what he wanted, he made his way down the passage and away from the direction from which Irie and Fred had come. He was, of course, checking that the bag did NOT contain dog poo but instead something else of interest. And that something else made Rafe as satisfied as far as he could be made satisfied, which was not much.

Fred had some information to share: "Irie, that was Rafe. You know, from High Storrs School. Year 13. I just found out my sister Melanie's stuck on him. He's the boy I saw disappear into the gennel."

Irie was not pleased, "Oh really? Now you tell me."

But Fred had more information. "Yeah. She helps him with his math and he acts like he's interested in her."

Irie now asked a key question, "Is he?"

Fred was amused. "My sister? Interested in my sister – Melanie? Well, there's no accounting for taste. BUT what he really wants, what he really desires is to get into St Bearnard's University in Scotland. Next year after he finishes year 13 and graduates from High Storrs School. Then he goes on a hunt for a future spouse. Someone who will provide entry into the financial elites of this fair and green land."

Now it was Irie's turn to be amused: "St Bearnard's where strolleth beneath the hallowed Scottish walls the poshos. The royal nieces and nephews. Cousins and second cousins in the dozens. And out to the nth degree."

Fred was happy to play along. "St Bearnie's is undoubtedly where some of the most aristocratic kids have earned their undergraduate degrees. Or found a spouse and dropped out. Excellent university for Scottish history and a very exclusive marriage market. If you're into that sort of thing."

Irie was coy. She pretended not to have heard about young men and women looking for life partners and even, perhaps, love – with the right sort of person Irie: "Marriage market? How did I not know that? So who is Rafe other than your sister's romantic target? And what is he doing here? Is he a bloke who gets excited by smelling dog poo? There are lots of strange guys in the world, if scary movies on TV are to be trusted – I know you have your doubts, but your sister can do better than that."

Hobgoblin was beginning to tire of this chit chat about the romantic feelings of humans, together with their strategies for landing marriages with this or that type of person. And so the goblin said, "Rafe is a nuisance stumbling about in the gennel tunnel on a daily basis. He always has a bag of dog poo that is clearly NOT a bag of dog poo. One would think he worked for the CIA or MI6, but he belongs to Grasshwort, the geomancer."

Irie suddenly remembered Hobgoblin's first statement to Fred. Irie: "So you knew we were coming? I could hear what you said to Fred when we were in the brick passageway." And then she knew that she had given away her bestest best friend's name, but she wasn't very worried because the conversation had been so pleasant and so – well the word that fits here is her mum's – "nice."

Hobgoblin addressed her question directly and in detail: "Yes, I knew someone was coming. Not exactly who but someone. Word gets around among my friends. Sometimes it's vague, but it does get around. There's the lady who sells the Mexican chocolate to me. You seem to know her. But she didn't say exactly who was coming to see me for gungoi and focaccia. Just two kids from the neighbourhood. A practical one with a strong heritage of sea- faring men of India. Lascars. She, a wise one, also with roots in another part of the world – Jamaica."

Fred went wide eyed. "That would be you, Irie. Maybe the Lascar heritage is not something you made up to sound like a person from a romance novel. Not puffery after all. And Jamaica. That's Windrush."

Hobgoblin continued, "The other, a reader of books. The history of this fair, green land. A lover of languages, old and new. But a funny thing: This one, a boy, is 'not from around here.' Well treated but not always on the guest list."

Irie decided to take on a sensitive topic: "Let's see, who do we know who might be a history boffin? Guest list?" Irie's voice filled with irony: "You're not really British like I am." The irony came from the fact that Irie was British and not British, a native of the British Isles but at the same time not quite an insider. And Fred the expat American? Another outsider. The two were, on this account, made for one another.

Fred spoke from shared experience, "But you put up with me even if I come from a land of barbarians. Americans may have piles of cash, but no fancy titles. In Yuma, we have lizards and Scorpians. Also a few Gila monsters." Hobgoblin first looked puzzled and but then strangely pleased by the thought of Gila monsters, so Fred continued, "Gila monsters are just big, fat, colourful lizards. But don't let one chew on your foot."

Hobgoblin responded, "If I ever visit Yuma, I'll wear thick boots." Irie thought about saying: "Definitely Doc Martins in your case" but let the moment pass and returned to the topic of outsiders.

Irie leaned her head to one side, coyly opened her eyes as wide as she could, and directed her remarks to Hobgoblin, "Freddie and I have our own parties and invite those worthy of our company. The insiders are the real the riff-raff. The hoi polloi, and we are very exclusive." She expected to do Classics in year 12, and had gotten a start with the word "hoi polloi." Then she got around to the question that she and Fred had been waiting to pop: "And who, pray tell, are you? We know that you can cook like Elizabeth David in a frenzy of creative energy, or even, banish the thought, the American chef James Beard. But who, in the name of all that's holy in haute cuisine, are you? Actually?"

Hobgoblin took a long breath and decided that he could trust the two friends. He did not hesitate further to reveal a good deal, though not everything, about himself. The goblin- chef started by saying: "And I? I am my name. A hobgoblin named Hobgoblin. Servant for so many centuries to the Fairy Queen."

Irie was thoroughly impressed. "Oh, I'd so like to meet her. The Fairy Queen. Does she have her court underground? Is she tiny or of regular size? Can she change and get big and small? And what clothing does she wear. Bodices and ruffs? Silver shoes with diamond buckles?"

Hobgoblin reluctantly but firmly dampened her enthusiasm. "You may desire an audience with the Fairy Queen but I won't be able to introduce you."

Fred was not afraid to inquire into what might be a delicate matter. Fred: "No? What happened?"

Because of his newfound trust in them, Hobgoblin was not afraid to confess. "I am banished from the Fairy Queen's court and from Fairyland itself. Banished. Some would say 'shamed,' but I will only admit to being banished."

Irie tried to be discreet, but still wanted to know more. Irie: "Banished for what?"

Fred, being Fred, blurted out: "For what crime?"

Irie: "Freddie Gustafson, for goodness sake."

Hobgoblin: "It was a crime. Pardonable, I think, but a crime."

Fred: "Cool! Probably not bloody, I'd hazard. No way that. Steeped in blood is not your thing, Hobbie."

Irie was livid. "Freddie Gustafson, you stop right now. Stop or I'll disown you. Do not say another word until I tell you to. And call people by their proper names until asked to do otherwise. Which won't happen in this case, I'd wager."

Hobgoblin continued as if he had not heard the two friends. He was, in fact, lost in a memory. Hobgoblin: "I petitioned Her Highness for a lovely new kitchen. Big stainless steel American fridge. Three kinds of bins: For recyclables, for kitchen waste, and for everything else – rubbish actually. The FQ flat out refused. 'No!' says she in a voice that would have turned all in her court to stone, if they were not used to her rages and so covered their ears.

'Ye shall not have it, impertinent wretch!' Wretch, mind you. She called me a 'wretch.' And 'impertinent.'"

Now both Irie and Fred fell silent, fell under the spell of Hobgoblin's story: "'Quartz counter top,' says I. 'One can ill afford this kind of extravagance for the sake of a mere hobgoblin cook,' says she.' 'Harrumph!' says I, and walks off the job right then and there. FQ pleading poverty. She has a claim on every acorn in Ireton Wood. Ask the squirrels and they'll tell you the amount of her take. American and Canadian squirrels, by the way. Mostly. Not many English red squirrels left in this part of her kingdom. Red squirrels? All gone north. And to call me a 'cook' a mere cook when I have enviable credentials as a chef. I'll show you my cordon bleu someday if we get to know each other better."

Hobgoblin paused for a second and Fred filled the gap: "My apologies for the American part in the squirrel invasion." As he said this, Irie caught his eye and frowned in the tiniest way. Fred caught the meaning immediately: "Not an apology, really. But I am sorry it happened. The thing with the squirrels. The American squirrels, only though. I can't say anything about the Canadian ones. Also, I may have come from Yuma, but I brought no rattlesnakes, scorpions, or Gila monsters, for that matter."

Irie thought that Fred was getting a little dramatic and in the process slowing the pace of Hobgoblin's story. Even breaking the spell of the narrative. Irie: "Can you do me a favor, Fred? Do we really want to know all about your lovely old home and picturesque life in the land of vast, empty deserts?"

Hobgoblin barely noticed the remarks from Fred and the spell was by no means broken. Hobgoblin: "So I agreed to come and work for the Geomancers Society. They arranged for the kitchen you see here. Best not to say too much about the "how" of the financing of that. What paid for it. But the Geomancers didn't call me 'wretch,' and I liked that. They never said 'impertinent." Respect. 'Mr Hobgoblin' is what they said. That's excessive. Don't use that on me, you two. No 'Mr' for you two. But it was nice on occasion. AND. The old man who's been using the gennel to come down here. The one who controls your friend Rafe using the dog poo bag. The ancient one with the green corduroy trousers and the muddy shoes. He's one of them. A Geomancer. Or used to be until they struck him off."

Now Irie now began to put two and two together. "We saw him. He was looking through binoculars near the Millhouses Park, near the RC boat pond. He was looking across the River Sheaf."

Fred chimed in, "Struck him off? Does that mean that they lifted the old dude's license? And he's a Geomancer? With a capital 'G.' In the Society? Oh, I mean 'Was in the society, 'till they pushed him out the door. I guess we should have known by looking at his shoes that he had that geomancer connection to clay and loam and all of that. Pretty scuffed and dirty, those shoes. That's a geomancer thing, geomancer with a small 'G.'"

Irie stopped the flow of commentary from Fred. Irie: "Freddie, what do you know about geomancers? I mean, really?"

Fred: "Only what I read in books."

Irie: "Sci fi and fantasy. Frederick, you are incorrigible."

Hobgoblin stroked his well-trimmed goatee, momentarily drawing the attention of Irie and Fred away from their set of set of silly remarks made to one another. Hobgoblin: "Come to think of it, Grasshwort is not fully struck off. He is on probation of some sort. Still has some powers. Not so great as before. Still in the Society."

Fred, however, was not quite ready to let go of his sparring with Irie. So to get in a dig at her he spoke as if he were a truly innocent boy and Hobgoblin was a much-respected male teacher. Fred: "'Incorrigible?' Sir. Irie really, really wants to have that that little chat with Her Highness. You know, the Fairy Queen. Ask Her Highness one-on-one where she buys her dresses. Where she gets her trinkets. Not the Primark, I'll wager." Primark was a discount store that Irie abhorred like the plague. For her it was COVID or more likely double COVID.

Irie knew he'd gotten her in their trivial, little back and forth, but she didn't care even a tiny bit. She was, to tell the truth, unabashedly pleased by the idea of meeting the Fairy Queen. Irie: "OK. OK. Freddie, I stand corrected. You know all there is to know about geomancers. What they wear. When and if they clean mud off of their shoes. Whether they wear wingtips. Brogans. Crocs. Crocs?

Would a real geomancer ever wear crocs? After all, crocs are easy to wash, to get the mud off. But not the right style." Irie paused and then went on: "But you, Freddie, you CAN have your grammar corrected. Indeed, SHOULD have your grammar corrected. You are not the great grammar guru. FINALLY. Freddie, don't call Mr Hobgoblin "sir." He's not a teacher at High Storrs School." Fred thought to himself but refrained from saying: "Maybe he should be a teacher at High Storrs. If he taught cooking, I'd take his classes. But then cooking is not an A-Level subject. Sigh."

Having disposed of the conversation with her bestest best friend, Irie turned to Hobgoblin. "Would it be possible? Her highness? I know you can't introduce me yourself because of the kitchen – Oh, US, not just me for the introduction. Me and Freddie, both – But maybe you know someone who's in her good graces. 'Grace and favour?' Is that the way you say it? Not on the outs with her highness. In the outs?"

Hobgoblin ignored the question and abruptly shifted the mood back to serious business. "And now we must speak of Orgone. I will give you directions so that you can find a certain large and dusty English country house. It is there that the Fairy Queen's garnet-covered gold cup is surely hidden. There are dangers to be faced. Dangers not so much of the physical sort. No, mostly serious dangers of thought and feeling. Emotion. Dangers posed by Orgone. Dangers that Orgone will place in your way. In the paths that you follow. Both of you."

Irie and Fred looked at one another and said together: "Yes, chef."

PART TWO

Chapter 1

Country House Life

Irie and Fred sat on piles of junk in a dusty country house on the afternoon of the day when they met Hobgoblin. People definitely would have called it junk, but to give it a history, it was what had been stored over the centuries first in this disused room and then in that. The junk was composed of stuffed birds in glass cases from the eighteenth century. Children's toys from the nineteenth century. Old, threadbare, powder-blue and white striped sofas and fainting couches from the 1920s. A worn baby carriage from the 1930s that was once called a "pram." Even in the dust, black lacquer gave it a diminished lustre. A red and white girl's bicycle with flat tires from the 1950s. In the midst of all of this, the two friends sat finishing off focaccia sandwiches. Hobgoblin had packed them lunches.

Truth to tell, the country house was dusty but not deep in dust and there were few spider webs. It wasn't particularly spooky and more like the large basement of an Oxfam or a Goodwill. Almost homey on that account. Still, there was no sign that anyone lived there or even stopped by to check on things more than every now and then.

Fred was perched on a swollen cardboard box, on which was written in black marker JOHN'S TOY TRAINS. Fred: "Hobgoblin was a dude to pack these sandwiches, Irie. He's one good chef. Focaccia bread and some sort of cheese. Excellent chutney."

If Fred was his usual cheery self, Irie was not in a good mood. The two had been rummaging around in piles of stuff for several hours and had come up with nothing. She was standing, leaning on a large oval mirror that had wooden legs and that could be tilted this way and that. Irie: "And not so nice of Hobgoblin to send us on this wild goose chase – looking for the Fairy Queen's stupid wine glass. This country house is like a monster flea market that can't sell anything. And do me a really big favor, would you? Stop calling Hobgoblin 'dude.'"

Rather than being offended, Fred found Irie's bad mood amusing. Fred: "Hey, I only called him dude once. Just now. So OK. Here's the rewrite: 'Hobgoblin was a good bloke to pack these sandwiches.' But let's get back on track. It's a garnet-covered, gold drinking cup. Not an ordinary wine glass. It's not glass. The Anglo-Saxons were exceedingly clever with red garnets and with gold. AND I saw a cabinet full of drinks glasses in the next room. Not the kind of glasses we're looking for. But maybe the FQ's cup is in one of the drawers. Safe from prying eyes."

Irie: "That would be too easy. Freddie, my good man." Irie was in the process of giving in to his good cheer.

Fred: "Hobgoblin made it sound like a quest. The Holy Grail."

Irie: "What he really meant was for us to go through somebody's rubbish. Somebody who was too lazy to load it up and drive it to the tip. And wasn't searching for the Holy Grail a death trap for a zillion odd knights of the Round Table? What happened to Sir Galahad? Wasn't he burned at the stake?"

Fred: "That was Joan of Arc. What a cool word for the city dump – the tip. And dumping in the forest is called fly tipping. But do you tip the junk out on the fly, while driving a pickup truck? Or do the flies look for lunch in what you tip out while driving in a pickup truck? What is the source in real life of the phrase 'fly tip'?"

Irie: "Stop it. NOW. I'll go by myself the next room to the wine-glass cabinet. You stay here and finish. But, you know, just the same I would like to meet her. The Fairy Queen. I'd want see her in a house that she keeps tidy. Take a peek in her wardrobe and jewellery boxes. Maybe examine her tea chest."

Fred was unable to resist a dig at Irie's fascination with the Fairy Queen. Fred: "What you really want to do is rummage through Her Highness's closet and try stuff on. Now you've found a mirror to use."

Irie posed in front of the mirror and put her head on one side to look fetching. She opened her eyes as big as she could.

Fred continued, "Tilt the mirror this way and that. Move it into the best light. You're probably too large for her clothes, anyway." Now, Irie was not a big person and Fred's well-meaning joke landed on deaf ears. Irie was not amused, but she adjusted the mirror and admired herself in it. Though she was wearing jeans and not a loose-fitting summer dress, she flounced around this way and that.

Irie: "Toxic masculinity raises its ugly head." She laughed but he knew that behind the laugh he had touched a nerve about elegant clothing and the Fairy Queen. He would try to be more careful I the future.

Irie: "It's natural for women to take an interest in what they wear. Not the least bit odd. And I'll go along with you. If the cup is not in this room, then it may be in the next in the cabinet." Again, she tilted her head on one side and coyly went on: "There may even be a brass-bound trunk in which there are ball gowns from the 1920s. Or flapper dresses. Headbands with long, tall feathers." She continued, "So, as I already said, on to the next room for me. You stay here."

Suddenly, it was Fred's turn to get moody. He said, "How many rooms does this house have?" Fred began to consider the danger that could be all around them. "What if Hobgoblin is lying to us? What if he is just going to keep us here going through this stuff forever? I really liked him. He seemed like a nice guy. Good food. BUT we didn't really know him. What's his stake in all of this? Why should he care if the Fairy Queen gets her cup back? And what about us? We might find it and send it to her and still be stuck here till the end of time. All without seeing her. All for nothing."

Irie countered his pessimism, "Hobgoblin said he would get us back to our families before we were missed. If we find the cup, we may get to see the FQ. If not, we are home in time for dinner. I don't think he would lie to us outright. Do you?"

Fred persisted, "No, I don't think Hobgoblin would lie outright. But I don't recall any promise about us getting an audience with Her Royal Highness. Hints and suggestions, maybe. Nothing we could claim as a promise. Just hints. AND I have a funny feeling, Irie. Really funny."

Irie began to experience the same sense of dread, but kept what she said upbeat and mildly sarcastic: "Something from one of your sci-fi novels?"

Fred ignored her sarcasm. "What if? What if time doesn't run the same for home as it does here in the country house. What if days here are only minutes back home? We'd not be missed for weeks. Months. Years."

Fred, without intending it, began to freak Irie. "Don't say that, Fredrick Gustafson. Don't be an idiot. You're such a twerp." She didn't think him a twerp. She was just getting upset. But, when she was upset, she always made a plan. Irie: "OK, here's what we're going to do. We're almost finished with the room we're in now. After we complete the one with the glasses' cabinet, we walk off the job. As I said, I go to that room. You stay here. And what we are talking about with rooms is not one of your infinite regresses. It's not an endless progression of rooms." She repeated with emphasis: "After the glasses' cabinet room, we call it quits. Cup or no cup. We're out of here."

Fred: "OK. Sacrée vache! What would we do without you to organize us?"

Irie: "Must you always spoil the moment with something from a French police drama?"

Fred: "Not actually. It just means "holy cow."

Chapter 2

Workin' on the Railroad

And so Irie made her way to glasses-cabinet room. Fred lifted boxes here and there to look under them. He pushed the shiny, black baby buggy to see if would still roll, and found that the wheels turned if he pushed down and forward. The contraption squeaked and flakes of rust fell on the floor under its wheels. Looking over the push bar of the pram, his eyes wandered back to the swollen cardboard box on which he had been sitting. As if from out of nowhere, the old kindergarten rhyme came into his head: "First comes love. Then comes marriage. Then comes a baby in a baby carriage." When that thought had passed, he considered the label in magic marker: JOHN'S TOY TRAINS. In his mind, he began to visualize a large, complex model railroad layout. Before long he turned thought into action.

Soon the floor around him was covered with track, some in bits and pieces and some connected into a small oval with a big bump on one side. Fred examined an engine and a few cars. They were parts of one passenger train. Then he set this rolling stock on the track and connected the bits to one another. The engine and the cars were all blue in the lower half, with cream tops. Some of them were marked with DB. Fred plugged in the controller and drove his passenger train around the layout a couple of times, after which he brought it to a halt and sat thinking for a minute. He next began to build a bridge, elevating the track with a pile of small wooden boxes that he found stacked together behind the baby buggy. Once the bridge was complete, he sat and watched the train go round and round, breathing regularly and falling into a sort of waking sleep. Irie entered and was puzzled by what she saw.

Irie: "What in heaven's name are you doing with that train set?" She spoke in a parody not just of her own mother but of mothers in general. It was a joke, but at the same time, he had been wasting time with a toy train like a child. "Must you sit there drottling?" If truth be told, Irie did not know what "drottling" meant but she was sure that this is what Fred was doing. She had picked up the word somewhere. And she by no means was wrong in its use.

Fred awakened from his half trance and said, "Drottling? What's that? This train set has got to be from the 1950s. But it works. And there's more track, another engine, and more . . ."

At this point, Irie interrupted. Irie continued to sound like someone's mother: "I've been away in the other room for less than two minutes and you've done all of this? I don't get it."

Fred, only half listening and still mostly focused on the train: "You've been gone for at least an hour. The controller is pretty crude. You can speed up and slow down but that's about it. Also the train motor is none too strong and the controller gets hot. It's really difficult when the engine tries to climb the incline to the bridge." Fred motioned to the bridge made of little wooden boxes. How could he have put together the track, tested the train, rebuilt the track over the new bridge all in two minutes?

Irie was becoming irritated but something about the bridge caught her eye. It was one of the small boxes, which seemed of better wood and better workmanship than the others. She could see that there was some sort of armorial crest and engraved initials, but she couldn't make out the details. She forgot about the differences in time that she and Fred had experienced.

Irie: "OK if I take this box out of the bridge and have a look?"

Fred didn't look up from his trains. "Why do that? You'll wreck my set up."

Irie was not going to be put off so easily. "I am not going to 'wreck' your little world of trains. I just want to look at the box. Now that's an elegant item, if ever there was one." Fred either did not hear her or was too caught up in the blue and cream cars snaking around the track to notice what she said.

Irie spied a box about the same size as the box she wanted, picked it up, and switched the two in the twinkling of an eye. The track was not dislodged and the whole setup was as before, just with a different box where the one with the armorial crest had been. Fred for a moment was not happy, but almost immediately went back to the revery of his train. Irie examined the box and its contents.

Irie spoke mostly to herself: "You know, I think I might just take this home for a jewellery box."

The box was made of mahogany and lined with red velvet. It contained an old two-shilling piece, a couple of small seashells, and what appeared to be three of someone's baby teeth, which were in a purple silk bag with a gold drawstring. Although the silk bag was in a depression in the red velvet, it didn't really fit there. Something else had been intended to fit into that spot. Irie, who really didn't notice any of this, emptied the silk bag into her hand.

Irie: "Fred, stop being a five-year-old with that train and take a look at this. Three baby teeth. Probably from long, long ago."

Fred stopped the train for a moment, and Irie took his hand, hoping to put the teeth into it. Fred quickly drew his hand back. Fred: "Stop trying to weird me out."

By now the afternoon was beginning to fade. The shadows in the room became longer and Irie said less with sarcasm and more with wistfulness, "Time to go home. We can come back and look for the Fairy Queen's lovely cup tomorrow. Which means tomorrow you can play with your trains. Actually, the colour scheme on the engine and coaches is quite pretty. So, turn off the gizmo and unplug the thing. Leave everything set up. Nobody's doing to disturb it. You may find a few new dust bunnies at the station tomorrow. They can be tumble weeds rolling around your tiny Yuma station."

Fred, who had started to reattach the controller to its cord, was too absorbed to hear her and Irie took a closer look at the crest on the box.

Irie: "There's a crest and initials: MIR. A lady's initials, for sure. Maybe Mary Irene somebody. Mary Irene Ragdoll." She laughed at her own joke.

He ignored it. "You should look at this." Suddenly the shadows got longer almost moving, if either of the friends had thought to look. As the room darkened, Irie flipped a switch on the wall, which turned on an art deco floor lamp. Then Irie noticed the time.

Irie: "OK, let's go."

Fred: "No way. There is plenty of light from the lamp."

Irie: "We have got to get out of here."

Fred: "Another ten minutes."

Irie: "OK, I am going back to the third room for a quick look. Five minutes. Then we head for home."

Fred: "Ten minutes. Sure thing. Fair princess. Tiny one."

Irie picked up Fred's backpack and put the box with the armorial crest into it. Zipped up the backpack, then unzipped it. Looked inside and said to herself, "MIR. A puzzle worth working on." Then she made her way through the junk and into the room with the cabinet and its glasses.

Chapter 3

Back to Hobgoblin's Kitchen

Irie and Hobgoblin looked at one another across the long oak table in his kitchen, she sitting on an ordinary wooden chair and he on a three-legged stool tall enough to bring him up to a level with her. She pushed the box with the armorial crest towards him across the glass top. He was hesitant but touched it lightly with the tips of his long fingers, while examining it carefully with his eyes and giving it small sniffs with his long nose. Irie, seeing him devoting his full attention to the box, took the opportunity to sneak a big chunk out of her focaccia sandwich. It was the sandwich that she brought from the country house, a sandwich still wrapped from the bottom in a sheet of brown baking paper. Hobgoblin took his time, and she had plenty of opportunity for a second bite, but she didn't venture it. Indeed, she had trouble chewing and swallowing what she had in her mouth.

After Hobgoblin finished his examination of the outside, he spoke, "Small child, would you kindly open this mahogany box for me? It is very ancient. From the time of Shakespeare and Queen Elizabeth the First." She waited for him to push it over to her, but when he did not, she reached across the table and pulled it to where she sat.

Hobgoblin was anxious and repeated himself nervously, "Open it, for me, please if you would."

Irie opened it.

Hobgoblin: "I may not touch the contends under severe penalty. I probably should not have examined the outside so thoroughly, but I needed to be sure." He paused and Irie put her focaccia sandwich down on the table. He then spoke again, "Irie, please tell me about your friend."

Irie began clear as a bell, but then had trouble getting the words out: "I went to the other room and poked around. After about five minutes, I went back to the room Fred was in but he couldn't see or hear me. And he had expanded his railway. There were little rivers and mountains. Where the bridge built of wooden boxes had been, now there was a model train bridge. Little steel girders. Completely like real life. I couldn't get into the room. I could only stand outside, right at the door fame. And he didn't see or hear me. So I came back to the gennel kitchen. I know you can help. Will you help? Please, sir."

Hobgoblin: "Young Fredrick has gotten himself into a peck of trouble, Irie. A mire, more-like, though not entirely of his own making. You shouldn't blame him too much. BUT he is going to have to stay in that room enjoying himself until he becomes bored. The trouble is that this particular room is very good at keeping people from becoming bored."

Irie felt cold and moist. She was smart enough to understand that this was going to be another time when she need to make a plan. But what sort of plan? All she could think of was how stupid Fred was being. Irie: "He'll never get bored of those trains. They kept getting nicer and nicer. They're a pretty colour and the world around them becomes more and more real. It's like a whole reality creating itself. Somehow, somehow, I don't think Fred is actually making it. It's too authentic. Too clean. The railway staff on the platforms are more like tiny people rather than plastic figures. I expected them to start walking around. Conductors helping old ladies with their luggage. Kids getting loose and running away from their mothers. It was too real. Too real."

Hobgoblin was pleased. Pleased that she anticipated what he was about to say: "Yes, Irie. This is not Fred. This is Orgone's work. A grand illusion. Orgone knows people's desires and fulfils them to their detriment. A descendent of Circe, this Orgone. But you don't want to know all of what's in that tale." This last, the idea that some pieces of information were being withheld from her didn't make Irie happy. And she did know about Circe from reading Percy Jackson. But not Orgone. Orgone was not in any of the Percy Jackson books.

Nevertheless, Irie didn't dispute openly with the small creature about Circe and didn't offer any change in her facial expression to indicate irritation about being denied the story of Orgone. She was resolved to be as pleasant as she could be, but she filed Orgone away in her mind. And she filed away Hobgoblin's withholding of information.

Hobgoblin continued, "The best news is this very old mahogany box that you have found. Found among the leavings of history, the dusty treasures of centuries stored in the country house. Dusty but not too dusty. Dusty enough for proof of age. But not quite dusty enough to go beyond fiction. Beyond history made tidy in a way that seems negligent but is not. So, to the point: You found the mahogany box and somehow knew how to remove it safely. Knew that you must take it. Your conscious thought was, to make it a jewellery box for yourself. But somewhere back in the back of your mind something else told you to zip it up into the young gentleman's ruck sack. And you escaped from the house with no difficulty. I could not have accomplished that. There would be no Hobgoblin had I been in the house and tried."

Irie suddenly developed new feelings about the container that she had planned to use for her stuff, her things, her funny little rings and bracelets, and whatever. If the truth be known, she wondered whether the result of her lugging the lovely little box away from the country house would lead to there being no Irie. Fred was right, maybe this once. The box with the armorial crest and its little velvet bag were creepy. She, herself, was getting creeped out.

Irie: "Can I keep it here in the kitchen with you? I don't really want to haul it home."

Hobgoblin was as emphatic as he could be and even harsh: "No." Irie was taken aback by Hobgoblin's tone, but then intrigued by what he said next: "There are some things that you can do that will help you to rescue the youth. You don't have to just wait for Fred to become bored. So, find a way to disrupt his pleasure. Be devious."

Irie thought to herself, "Be devious?" Her first reaction was, "Devious? That is simply not me. I don't do that sort of thing." But then, as she considered it more, she admitted to herself that she could be devious when what she wanted was important enough. Not just that she wanted it a lot. But when it was important. Maybe with just a touch of want or even desire. But the base had to be importance.

Hobgoblin took a reassuring tone: "Now it is time for you to go back to Sheffield. Only a few minutes will have passed from when you first entered into the gennel. And another thing . . ." Hobgoblin took a little time to consider what he would say next.

While he was mulling over his exact words, Irie suddenly blurted out, "You keep the box. I don't want it." She surprised herself by her harsh, impolite tone.

The harshness in her tone made it easier for Hobgoblin to reveal what he needed to reveal: "No, Irie, you must carry it. The mahogany box is from a royal palace of Fairyland. It is a casket. As I said, I should not be touching it. And likewise, it is not good for it to remain here with me. For me to be its keeper. I am sorry to say this or to say it this way, but the box is your burden."

Irie, without showing it, became confused for a moment. Hobgoblin made carrying the box sound like a heavy responsibility, something she would not like. And that was how she felt before. But now her mood started to shift and she became strangely, quietly joyful. Here was something belonging to the royal palace. Maybe to the Fairy Queen herself. Queen Mab. Quite suddenly she discovered that she knew that name. Mab, the queen. But how? How did she know? Not from reading, not from conversation with Fred. How?

As Irie stood up, absorbing what Hobgoblin had said, he spoke again from his tall stool at the table, repeating what he had said earlier: "Now it is time for you to go home to Sheffield. Only a few minutes will have passed from when you first entered into the gennel.

And another thing . . ."

That word, "home" gave Irie solace, courage, and an emotional reservoir of strength.

What Hobgoblin said next, confirmed her in a serene feeling of power: "You are going to get Fred out of that room with the trains. He may become a little bored on his own. But he will need a nudge from us, a distraction. Well, a nudge from you and not me."

For a moment Irie thought: "Am I being used by this hobgoblin for his own purposes." With a touch of sarcasm she started to politely interrogate him: "What nudge? What do you mean?"

And then she found herself furious when Hobgoblin continued, "I cannot tell you."

But before she could explode in anger, he concluded, "I cannot tell you because I don't know what nudge you will give the young gentleman. Perhaps a remembrance, a token of yourself in some way, from a distance. What remembrance, what token, I do not know. But I do know that you will discover that nudge. Or I think you'll make that discovery. No, I am sure. Still. . ." Hobgoblin didn't sound convincing and his voice trailed off.

Irie, however, was filling with confidence as she observed her own mind, which she found filling with plans. She was sorting and sifting a pile of actions that she might take even as she was talking to the little creature. Tossing out some plans. Saving others for later. She was almost ready to make firm choices.

Reading Hobgoblin a little like a book, Irie paused from thinking and said, "But you had something else in your mind. What was it?"

Hobgoblin, for his part, was delighted with what in other circumstances he would have considered a cheeky question, "That right there is a good sign. You have a sharp eye and a keen ear. You can read my thoughts, not always, but sometimes. So, here's what I was thinking, what I needed to tell you: When you emerge from the gennel, nobody will quite recall Fred. You will have clear knowledge of him, of course. But nobody else, including his mother and father. They will only hazy memories. Not even his older sister, the math boffin. It will be as if he never existed or exists in some sort of fog."

Irie was not really surprised. "Fred guessed something like this might happen. Time and space. But down to basics. I will enter the corbelled passageway, walk to the end where there's a white limestone wall. That limestone with its black spots. Mold or something. And there must be a word to say. Something in Anglo-Saxon except not 'something' because that's the word that got us in. So the word 'nothing' gets us out. Maybe."

As Irie turned and walked to the door that led into the passageway, Hobgoblin said after her, "Your young gentleman friend is fortunate to have such a wise young woman to look after him."

Although she would have considered it hugely impolite in any other circumstances, Irie did not turn and say "thank you" or "good-bye." Not even looking at him, she put the backpack on the floor and took out Henry Sweets Anglo-Saxon dictionary. She paged through it. Made a mental note of something, and then simply marched ahead into the corbelled passageway.

Chapter 4

Nanwiht

Using the light of her mobile phone, Irie carefully watched her feet for places where they could be caught in the floor of the corbelled arch passageway. It wasn't long before she reached the limestone wall, where she put down the backpack and took out Sweet's Anglo- Saxon Grammar, checking to see if her memory was correct about the entry on "nothing."

Irie thought to herself: "I memorized 'nan thing,' but it says here that it could also be 'nanwiht.' Any reason to try one or the other first? Maybe both work. Maybe both work for different purposes. In different ways. Maybe neither works. Jeez Louise. Too much thinking. Chant 'nanwiht' three times and see what happens."

And that's what she did. NANWIHT. NANWIHT. NANWIHT. The result was that she found herself beginning to come into focus at the bend in the gennel. She peered down at her hands and feet as they came into sharper and sharper focus. Quite an experience, she thought. But, rather than play the part of a fool and stand there resembling nothing so much as a fence post planted in the ground, she casually walked over the stone bridge, and chose to take the proper path rather than the shortcut through the stickery holly bushes. She probably didn't need to be especially careful regarding the rules of the woodland paths, but playing safe allowed her to reassure herself. The choice of route meant that she made her way home in that early afternoon by passing near the Q Pit.

There sitting on a fallen log and a large stone were Simon Grasshwort and Rafe. The two stopped talking when they saw Irie on the main path. For her part, she was immediately curious that this pair were talking together. Both had something going on in connection with the gennel, and she would have liked to know what it was. At the same time, she didn't want to do the gormless thing and smile cheerfully while offering the Sheffield greeting, "Hi-ya?"

So, she briefly looked over at them, placing her gaze about a foot above their heads. Fred had told her that this is what Navajos do when they don't want to make eye contact. She found that it worked at High Storrs School when a head boy or girl became too full of him or herself.

Now the biggest problem for Irie was a particular temptation. She would have absolutely loved to conceal herself behind a holly bush to overhear all of what these two were discussing. But that would have led to her exposing herself as a mark-one idiot.

So she walked on.

Rafe hardly noticed her, because, while he had seen her at High Storrs School on numerous occasions, she was two years below him and hence only visible as an invisible person. Grasshwort, however, was considerably more astute than the young fellow who was gunning for St Bearnard's University. The man of the muddy shoes noticed her slight hesitation as Irie decided to not look at him but above him. People do not do that sort of thing, he thought to himself, without a good reason. She continued to amble down the path in a manner that also seemed unusual, perhaps too casual for a normal stroller in the woods. Rafe wanted to start talking as soon as Irie was out of sight. Grasshwort merely smiled and did not engage until he had scanned the holly bushes.

Rafe: "Grasshwort, are you getting spooked? You're not talking. And do we have a deal or no deal? No messing about."

Simon Grasshwort, seeing that nobody was eavesdropping, shifted into business mode. And he did not give any hint to Rafe of his suspicions about the girl on the path, the girl who was Irie. Grasshwort: "When you sit the A-Level exams, Rafe, I can get you more time, not a lot but some. Enough to make the difference. And we have to talk quickly now, while the Geomancer Society is having its monthly meeting. We cannot be seen together by anyone from the Society, or I will lose the little power I have to help you."

Rafe: "You are absolutely paranoid. And I'm finished with communicating through slips of paper in fake dog poo bags. Give me the details fast and I am gone before your ancient bloody brotherhood finishes its meeting and its munchies. Someone calls for 'the good of the order.' Gavel goes 'clunk.' All over."

Rafe was pleased with his own witticisms. Grasshwort: "But you must keep your side of the bargain. You must free my wife. You must trick Hobgoblin into lifting his spell. And remember, the dog poo bags were your idea. Actually pretty ingenious but at the same time over the top."

Rafe: "Like you told me to, I went in there to steal a loaf of his focaccia bread. But there was no door. No kitchen."

Grasshwort: "Hobgoblin, the little creature who dresses so oddly, he clearly knew you were coming and barricaded the door with an illusion. You could have walked in, but then how to get the focaccia without him knowing? He was supposed to be gone. I know his schedule, and he usually keeps to it. This time he didn't. He has something going on. He has had some visitors. I wish I knew who. The little creature in his skinny jeans and fancy shoes from London thinks he is a 'hep cat.' He may dress like a fool but does not think like one."

Rafe: "Well, I'm sorry. I tried. I don't see that there is anything else I can do. You have to help me with the A-Level exams anyway. It's the only honest thing for you to do. Honor your bargain. Skinny jeans, expensive shoes? This bloke sounds like hipster and not whatever it was that you said."

Grasshwort thought to himself. He put his head in his hand and looked like he was going to go to sleep. Rafe believed for a moment that Grasshwort had been nipping on a pint of vodka. For Rafe, Grasshwort looked like a year 13 boy about to pass out. Grasshwort came out of his revere with new information: "That girl that walked by us. I am remembering her. She will be able to help us with the focaccia. We, you and I, will find a way around the small "hipster" with the well-trimmed goatee. Hep cats are a dying breed. The ones that aren't dead are in care homes."

Rafe: "So, I still don't get it. Why a chunk of some sort of bread? You are never going to make any sense. And I don't care, as long as I get the extra time on the A-Levels."

Grasshwort decided to play a little game. "Hobgoblin has a weakness. Can you guess what it might be?"

Rafe was in no mood to play games. "Why would I? I really have better things to think about."

Grasshwort persisted, "It's pretty obvious – food. He loves cooking. Bitter orange tarts, gungoi. All that sort of thing. But most especially he prides himself on baking focaccia bread. And it's good. That bread."

Rafe was becoming thoroughly bored. "OK. So what?"

Grasshwort: "My wife, Elaine by name, was turned into a sparrow by Hobgoblin. Why? Because she left half a bowl of Hobgoblin's gungoi unfinished in a beechwood bowl on that hipster table in his kitchen. She had forgotten an appointment and was racing towards the exit when she was metamorphosed into a bird like a character out of Ovid's Metamorphoses."

Rafe: "Who's Ovid? Oh, forget it. I don't care." Rafe sat for a moment and then came up with his answer to the reason for stealing the focaccia: "So your wife left Hobgoblin to do the dishes. I wouldn't be happy either. By the way, I don't think I'd leave her alone with that little twit if I were you."

Grasshwort: "I don't suppose you've heard of Percy Jackson? Greek Myth. Ovid was a Greek myth maker." At this point Rafe stood, put his hands in his pockets, and shuffled. The old man of the muddy shoes paused to give Rafe a chance to consider the question of Hobgoblin's motives. Now, Rafe was often dismissive of the thinking of other people when he should not have been. But he was not completely stupid.

Rafe: "Oh, I get it. He thought your wife was a food snob and turned up her nose."

Grasshwort: "Bang on target – or maybe close enough. So how do we get our little goblin to lift his spell?"

Rafe: "You tell him that she wants to come to lunch."

Grasshwort: "You are on the right track, but you haven't got it quite exactly. Here's what we do: we find another way for you to obtain a portion of Hobgoblin's famous focaccia bread. You feed it to my marital sparrow, she turns into a human, and I am once again a happy geomancer husband."

Rafe: "But doesn't the hipster need to see her eating the bread?"

Grasshwort: "Not at all. Hobgoblin will know the moment that his focaccia is eaten by Elaine. She could be sitting on a park bench in Iowa City and he'd know."

Rafe was not sure but thought that Iowa City might be famous for its potatoes. Rafe: "I still don't get it."

Grasshwort: "Elaine loves focaccia and when she eats it – when she enjoys it – Hobgoblin will know. His heart will melt and she will return to life as my lovely spouse – in human form. No more bird hopping around." He had told Rafe the word that would open the door to the kitchen, hwaethwegu. By using that word, Rafe would not feel like a fool looking at a soft and most wall made of Roman brick. So it was that Rafe could enter the kitchen but Rafe was now a little worried about keeping his own clean-cut good looks. Or at least that was Rafe's view of his appearance.

In point of fact Rafe suspected that he, himself, might be changed into some sort of ugly little bird. Or, more horrible, a plain one, like a wren. Oh, my god! Rafe: "So I have to take my chances by going back to the hipster kitchen. I'm not doing it. You can't make me and you still have to deliver on the A-Level exam."

Grasshwort: "No my boy. There is a girl who has just the sandwich that you need in her backpack. I think you'll find that she is on her way to a certain bench in Millhouses Park. A bench under a sessile oak. She is on her way home, but she will stop there to collect her thoughts and feel a kinship with someone not present." If Rafe were a little more curious about what was happening, he might have asked Grasshwort how he knew all of this about the girl from year 11 at High Storrs School, the invisible girl who now merited being visible. But Rafe had his eye on the prize.

Rafe: "So I go to the bench in Millhouses Park. Find her. I say I'm hungry. She looks at me. She gets excited and offers me the sandwich. I take it and bring it to you."

Grasshwort did not say a word, leaving the matter to Rafe to manage. But Grasshwort did think to himself: "You might have better luck if you just steal the backpack."

Chapter 5

Two Loo Visits

Fred sat behind a large console in the passageway between three rooms of the junk-filled country House. This was a console of the sort one might imagine finding at a regional branch of the UK's Network Rail, though in a smaller version. Various trains moved in and out of three rooms. There were tiny tunnels, rivers, bridges, and all sorts of wonderful bits relating to model railroading. The passenger cars were blue and cream and all had the letters DB on them, which signalled that they belonged to Deutche Bahn. But this was not a railway of the present day. Rather it was a German railway of the 1950s. Had Irie been there, she would have sworn that she saw the conductor helping an elderly lady with baggage.

But Irie was not there. Nor was she at the bench under the sessile oak, for, while Grasshwort could read her mind when he was in his trance, she could change that same mind after he had reappeared to talk with Rafe. And that is what had happened. So where was Irie?

Irie was in serious discussion with Lady Yerba on the front porch of the house with the avocado-green toilet. The discussion was not so serious that a few jokes or ironic remarks were excluded from what they were saying, and they were comfortably seated at COVID distance in the old aluminium lawn chairs with woven plastic seats and backs. Irie, who had rubbed her hands with disinfectant, never before had been sat in the chair that faced Lady Yerba, and she wondered if this wasn't a bit like going to the school psychologist.

"Had been sat," Irie thought to herself. Fred, the American, would never have said that. Thought that. As a matter of fact, Irie had been invited to visit the psychologist from time to time and had taken up the offer once. Clearly there was a chair in the shrink's office that was used for pupils who had profound emotional difficulties but also for those just needing some help in sorting out their lives. A shrink could be helpful, even essential – with family matters, academics, kids of the opposite sex. That sort of trouble.

Lady Yerba lifted a long black strand of hair from where it had fallen in front of an eye. "Hobgoblin is right. You need to find a way to free your companion. And don't hate Fredrick for getting himself into this. People have desires. Boys have desires. And don't hate him if you find that unexpected desires twist and wind around like tendrils in his mind."

Irie was amused by the mystery of "unexpected desires" because she knew, or thought she knew, the sort of boy that Fred was, not really interested in girls in the same way lots of year 11s were. She thought about one sort of girl at school. The rough kids called them 'chavs' and many other kids thought that word was not OK. These girls would call Fred an idiot, or, if they were in a good mood, "tame." Tame was a serious insult.

Irie rose from her aluminium chair and said, "I still have to get him released from the room that's overstuffed with toy trains. I think he might fall in love with a little bridge or a tunnel before he would . . ." Irie dismissed this line of thinking and went on to more immediate matters.

The reason that she had stood up became apparent when she spoke, "I need the loo. Back in a flash." Irie crossed the porch towards the front door but paused to examine a flowerpot, in which she found a very large, strikingly coloured snail. The head of the snail was out of its shell and the eye stalks were extended. It seemed to be looking at her. Irie gave the snail something a little more than a glance, hastily entered the house, used the loo, and returned. On the way back the snail was inside its shell. All that showed was wonderful whorls of yellow and black. Irie had wanted to meet its gaze.

Irie did not sit back down in the aluminium chair and instead spoke while standing: "Is he ever going to need the toilet? Everybody does. I just did. I mean he can't just play."

Lady Yerba, still placidly seated, said with a small twinkle in her eye, "Perhaps you should send him a toilet if you think he needs one. A friend would do that."

Irie caught on immediately, but spoke with hesitation, "Could I? I mean it's your sacred pool. How would I get it into the room with the trains? How would I get it back here?"

Lady Yerba: "You wouldn't need to send the thing itself. You could convey the phantasm of it. Friends often share thoughts and thoughts are made of images. Phantasms are a sort of thought. They, too, partake of the world of images."

For a moment Irie was spooked by the business of "phantasms" and their relationship to friends and the thoughts that occupy the minds of friends. Images and all that. But she didn't let it bother her too much, and she made her plan so fast that she hardly knew what she had done.

And then, she acted. She strode to the toilet/cenote and held the toe of her Converse so that it tightly connected the side of the bowl. Almost like an electric plug in a socket. All the while she was thinking of Fred as hard as she could. And that was not too difficult to do, since she had been thinking about Fred almost constantly since she left Hobgoblin's kitchen. What surprised her was the tingling that she felt in her toes on the foot that was in contact with the cenote. Almost electric. Now, she had tapped that avocado-green mysterious pool dozens of times as a favour to Lady Yerba and as a way to pick up just a tiny amount of magic, the sort of thing that would make you invisible when you stood under a lychgate. But she had never felt that tingling before. In any case, she knew that the phantasm would soon find its way to Fred.

She knew what he would do when he saw it. And she knew that she liked the tingling in her toes. It was a good feeling.

The toilet itself became a very pale white. It was no longer avocado green.

***

Fred stood up from his train console and stretched his arms. Like someone who has been nudged awake after being asleep for a long time, he stiffly walked away from the three rooms with the trains, away from his console and down the passageway. He tried several doors, just finding more junk in each room, until he came to one that opened onto a large bathroom with a tub set on four griffin's feet. The yellow and lavender striped wallpaper was peeling. There was a window high on the back wall, and the phantasm of the green toilet/cenote stood under it. Without giving the business much thought, Fred raised the seat and did a wee. Then he flushed. Water splashed in the toilet, circled around, and disappeared.

Fred's brain began to amp up, as if he were becoming fully awake. Fred: "Why the green toilet? Just like the one at Lady Yerba's." And then he thought, for the first time in a good long time, about Irie. He tapped the phantasm of the cenote/toilet with his foot, and slowly there, revealed before him, was a dusty and stained white art nouveau toilet. The phantasm was on its way back to Lady Yerba's front garden. Fred shuddered, but he again thought about Irie, this time with longing. Wishing she were there so they could talk about what had just happened but also to just talk and hear each other's voices.

Out in the passageway there was something else unexpected. All the trains had vanished, rivers and bridges. Back in the room where he and Irie had talked so much, there was the swollen cardboard box marked JOHN'S TOY TRAINS just as before the illusion. All that was missing was the mahogany box that Irie had taken with her. The station and the conductor helping the elderly lady with her elegant luggage was no longer there. This was room where it all began. He sat down on a blue striped fainting couch and began to shake.

Fred: "How could she do it? How could Irie leave me here in the middle of an illusion. That's what it was. An illusion now vanished. How could she desert me? Her friend." He might have been one of the foolish knights who had been obsessed with finding the Holy Grail. Irie had been right about that story from King Arthur's knights, if not in all of its details then in its general meaning. And then he thought that surely this was the work of Orgone. Fred had been tempted like Gawain. But then he thought again. Gawain was not tempted by toy trains. Gawain had been tempted by pleasant banter with a lovely woman.

Chapter 6

A Focaccia Sandwich

It was the day after she had left Fred in the deserted country house and Irie was sitting on their bench, the one under the sessile oak and with the orange lichen patch at one end. She had gone back to the stone bridge and had chanted "hwathwegu" three times but wasn't able to get the rhythm right. Or maybe that word only worked at certain times of day. Or something. In any event, she did not dissolve and reappear in the corbelled arch passageway. For once, she didn't have a plan and she was disconsolate. It was also clear that while Lady Yerba would offer hints from time to time, she did not want to unload this task from Irie. When the word "task" entered Irie's mind, it was soon followed by "burden." With that thought, she reached into a pocket in Fred's backpack, extracted mahogany box, opened it and looked inside. Another burden. That's how Hobgoblin had put it.

Then she saw Rafe approaching and quickly put the box back into the backpack. She extracted the now-stale focaccia sandwich and pretended to be eating lunch. There was, of course, one bite out of it already. Rafe strolled up to her as if they were old friends and sat down.

Rafe, radiating self-confidence, chuckled, and said, "Can I have a nibble?"

Irie: "Who are you? I don't know you. Go away."

Rafe: "You do know me. We both go to High Storrs School. I'm two years above you."

Irie made the mistake of setting Rafe straight about his and her status at the school. "Not so much two years above as two years older."

He took this come back as proof of their friendship. Rafe: "I love a saucy wench. Tease me more you spirited little vixen."

Irie: "Oh yes, I remember you now. You're Fred's math boffin sister's sorta-kinda-maybe boyfriend. Posho boyfriend. And I recall that you have a devil of a time keeping up in maths classes. You'll never get an offer of a place from St Beanie Uni if you don't put your nose to the grindstone and do a little maths homework. Without help from anyone. Who's going to be in the room with you when you sit A-Level exams? Not Freddie's big sis."

Rafe: "Fred who?"

Irie: "Fredrick Gustafson, of course. You and his sister. Yeah?"

Irie suddenly went silent as she twigged to the fact that Rafe would have forgotten the existence of Fred if he had ever known him. While Fred was still in the country house, nobody would remember him. For his part, Rafe was always up for a bit of his favorite activity: Lets Play Games

With the Truth. Or under its other name, Catch Me if you Can.

Rafe: "Oh, yeah. I know Fred. I used to coach his cricket team. Good player. He was from Ireland. Funny accent." Irie had placed the focaccia sandwich on the bench between herself and him. Rafe pointed at it with a sly wink. A wink that had in it a touch of lechery. Irie had listened to the lie, listened to the outrageous suggestion that based on his accent Fred was Irish rather than American, but she gave Rafe a little smile as if to say, "Go ahead, I'm finished with it. It's a nice sammy, but I wasn't really hungry." Rafe lunged for it. Gobbled it. Snarffed it. Scoffed it like a mad man. Soon the focaccia was all gone, except for some large crumbs that rolled under the bench on the end with orange lichen. The end where Rafe was sitting.

And then without quite knowing what she was doing, Irie caught herself, regretted that she had been the least bit polite to this outrageous oaf. And "nice sammy?" Why use that word that her mother liked so much? Why did she do that?

Irie: "Are you crazy? Fred never played cricket. He likes baseball. He doesn't have an Irish accent. That's American, not Irish. Don't you know the difference?"

For his part, Rafe realized that he had eaten the very object that he was to use to trade with Grasshwort for extra time on the A-Level exam. Rafe exploded: "Grasshwort grizzle guts. Pillock brains. Old git. Stinking warty. He owes me that time on the A-Level exams and I'm going to

116

get it. I tried my best, my honest best for that stale, mouldy sandwich. That's all anyone can ask." Irie had no idea what he was fuming about. A-Level exams. Her focaccia sandwich? It seemed he had gone mad. Nuts. Mad or sane, he stood and marched away without saying a word to her. She didn't feel hurt, but rather relieved. And, of course, puzzled. She did, however, enjoy the fact that Rafe had an orange stain on the seat of his jeans, and she imagined what the other boys in year 13 would say about it. Questions about what he had had for lunch. Whether he needed a trip to the loo. A check-up at the local surgery, perhaps with a lady doctor doing the exam. Combine with a check for polyps? Witticisms which would escape Rafe until someone broke down and told him. And that would only make things worse.

And so Irie's speculations about Rafe's pals from High Storrs School ended, and there she was once again sitting alone on a bench where she should have been sitting with her friend. There wasn't much reason for Irie to stay where they shared so much: the histories of their families, what each of them looked like, skin colour, eye colour, and whatever else. The girl who was famous for smart decisions and cool under pressure, simply could not think of anything to do. Any action to take. So she headed back to Lady Yerba's house, not so much in hopes of finding help but wanting company.

As Irie passed the red pole of a mail box, she thought of Freddie running at it. And then, she thought about his little chocolate frogs. If she kept on with this sort of thing, she would end up in a morass of self-pity, and self-pity was the kind of thing that she indistinctively avoided. Or tried to avoid.

When she arrived at the bottom of the driveway at Lady Yerba's, she could see that the toilet/cenote was back to its original avocado-green colour. Irie raced up the broken concrete of the drive, stopped, stood and looked at Lady Yerba: "The phantasm's back. He used it. Did a wee. The illusion of the trains must be gone? Am I right? And he knows he's not in a good spot. I wish I were there with him."

Lady Yerba: "I expect it was quite a surprise when the phantasm disappeared and what Fred saw before him was an art nouveau toilet. Very white, very expensive in the 1930s, but now woefully dusty and stained. The trains are gone and he is alone. He is sad. He is unhappy."

Irie found herself becoming annoyed with Lady Yerba. Was he, Freddie, to blame for getting himself into the mess he was in? No. But Lady Yerba made it sound like he deserved that mess. Clearly, that was not what the old lady was saying, but she was still annoying. And then, it jumped into Irie's head. The word. "Bruja." The old witch. Irie could scarcely believe what she was thinking about lady with the long black hair, the woman who had taught her a few little tricks of magic. But why? Why didn't Lady Yerba have a plan for her, one based on the superior knowledge – knowledge that let her see what Irie couldn't see. The disappearance of the trains. The boy alone and unhappy. Her friend. Not Lady Yerba's.

Lady Yerba: "Come and sit across from me. I will get you some chocolate made with boiling water. Good chocolate from Mexico. Use a little of the hand disinfectant. I will do the same before I handle your cup." And so Lady Yerba left the porch for her kitchen and Irie remained there alone sitting in the aluminium chair that was always there across from where Lady Yerba sat. That now, with COVID, was two meters away.

And yet, Irie was not alone. As she sat in the chair, she watched the snail with the yellow and black whorls climb the back of a terracotta frog. When it reached the top of the head, the snail turned and looked at her with its long eyestalks peering directly at her. And that look gave Irie a sense of peacefulness that she had not had in the presence of the kindly, well-meaning lady of much knowledge and many powers. Irie felt a kinship with this tiny creature and did not know why.

Back on the bench that belonged to Irie and Fred, the bench under the sessile oak, the oak with its limbs like twisty arms and the ends of its branches like fingers, there was a small bird on the ground. It was a house sparrow and it was pecking at crumbs of focaccia.

Chapter 7

Back at the Q Pit

Rafe sat across from Simon Grasshwort at the Q Pit. They were in the same places where they had been when Irie saw them the day before, and Rafe was loudly making himself out to be the victim of a scheming woman. That horrible girl had lured him to the bench at Millhouses Park. First she offered him the sandwich, and then laughed fiendishly and ate it herself in front of him. She began by calling the sandwich a "sammy" as if he and she were friends. Well, she might think they were friends but they definitely were not, not after what she had done. Now it was time for Rafe to turn his wrath on the man of the muddy shoes.

Rafe: "I need that extra time on the A-Levels exam and you have to give it me. I tried my best and that filthy girl – she ate it all in front of me for spite. Every last crumb."

Grasshwort found their conversation amusing and was not very convinced by the story of the evil girl. "Every last crumb. Are you sure? Is there a chance that she was a messy eater? Perhaps the situation is not so dire as you think."

Rafe: "My god how I hate that girl. No better than a chav. Next time I see her, she'll have been to the doctors for lip filler. But I shouldn't hate her because she's just useless. Worth zero. A bag lady in training. Not really up to being a chav. That's what she'll be if she succeeds in growing up. A bag lady sitting on a park bench. Making up non-existent people. Though I'll give her credit. I almost did remember. I almost believed her lies about some kid from year 11. Someone who probably doesn't even know her. Someone she has a crush on. A loser. Both of them losers. Now I remember. He's a criminal. Escaped from some place in America."

Grasshwort repeated himself, as if giving Rafe a clue in a crossword puzzle, "She is perhaps messy too, not a careful eater. Has a tendency to drop food on the floor, the ground."

Rafe knew that Grasshwort was doing a send up of some sort. The old git thought he was being funny: "What are you getting at, Grass Man?" Rafe's tone of voice was threatening.

Rafe stood and moved an inch or two towards Grasshwort, but then stopped as an elderly woman appeared on the path taking the same route that had been taken by Irie the day before. Unlike Irie, this woman turned from the path and advanced towards the Rafe and Grasshwort. She was casually dressed though in expensive clothing and her walking shoes were likely something she picked up at one of the high-end high-street shops on a London visit. She said, "Simon, this must be the boy about whom you spoke. The boy who is a little wayward. Not a bad child, but a little misguided." Grasshwort looked like he was going to approach her and even give her a quick hug.

Before the hug could take place, Rafe spoke, "OK, I know who you are, Mrs. Grasshwort. Your husband promised me extra time on the A-Level exams and you need to make sure he keeps his word. Make him be honest. I don't think he's a bad bloke. But he needs a firm hand from someone in charge. And that, pretty clearly, is you. Clothing says everything. You have class. And it's class that counts."

Elaine Grasshwort: "You should listen to your teachers and then converse in a meaningful way with your classmates. Learn the material. Develop the skills. Especially in mathematics, which, though a difficult subject, will come in useful later in life. And then, of course, there are the soft skills. Knowing how to listen and respond appropriately. Controlling anger and feeling empathy. Although, I will say that empathy is in short supply in this fallen world of ours." She said "fallen world" with a twinkle in her eye.

Rafe had a good deal of experience with teachers telling him that this or that was inappropriate behaviour, and it was not experience that he liked. He moved forward towards Elaine, coming within the two meter-COVID distance and speaking in his best soft, intimidating way: "Don't you talk down to me, mother Grasshwort."

Elaine Grasshwort smiled in a pleasant way and took a step backward. "If you're worried about the exams, don't be. I was only offering advice about the usefulness of really learning subjects in school and about social skills. Not about exams. I'm surprised that you don't know this already, but – there won't be any A-Level exams this year. COVID."

Rafe took a breath and stepped back himself. He didn't know whether to leap for joy because he was free from the A-Level exams or to turn and walk away in disgust because he had been caught out as unaware of a very important piece of information.

Elaine Grasshwort: "No way to sit exams this year without children being infected with the virus. I hope you have been turning in your homework, because that's what teachers are going to be using to give you marks."

Rafe suppressed the desire to tell Mrs Grasshwort what an overdressed French poodle she was. And that turned out to be a wise move, as he almost immediately remembered where he had seen her. The school district office. An administrator. She was in charge of something for all of the Sheffield schools. Student disciplinary cases? He couldn't remember. Or maybe she was the one who helped you get into the university you wanted if you were ambitious. Oxford, Cambridge. St Beanies's, definitely the Bean. Oxbridge was OK, but the real money and real social status was to be found elsewhere.

Elaine Grasshwort: "The announcement of the cancellation will be made on the evening news today, but most of your classmates know about it already. You must have seen some happy faces today and wondered."

Rafe: "I would have found out tonight on Zoom. There's a girl that's stuck on me, has it bad. She would have told me. Melanie." And then Rafe asked pretty much nobody but himself: "Doesn't she have a brother? Got into trouble with the police?" The truth of the matter was that Melanie would have teased him a judicious amount before giving him the happy news.

Grasshwort: "Well it's a bit of good luck for you. And this development in the UK schools means that our dubious deal can be forgotten. No harm done. No hard feelings." The man of the muddy shoes held out his hand in a gesture of a business deal done. Not entirely nice business deal (as Irie's mother might have said) but a business deal.

Rafe was not quite ready to let go of his anger, and he felt the best way to insult Simon Grasshwort was to take a shot at Elaine to whom he spoke as if Simon were not present. "Well, your husband will be deep in the dog poo without a plastic bag when the Geomancers find out about our little chat here. And they will find out because there is no Geomancer meeting on now. They finished it just as you came strolling down the path."

Grasshwort: "Would you be so good as to tell him, Elaine?"

Elaine Grasshwort: "My dear husband just finished typing his letter of retirement from active participation in the society. He will be an emeritus." She shot Grasshwort a sweet smile.

Elaine and Simon continued to converse with each other like a couple of elderly love- birds. Grasshwort: "We rent an allotment that we have not properly cultivated in years. A tidy little garden patch on shared public land. Indeed, there was some fear that we might lose it to other renters. But now we can enjoy ourselves."

Rafe found this sort of conversation boring and his mind was now churning with new ideas about how to deal with university admissions. Nevertheless he saw an opportunity to make a snide remark: "Typing? On a typewriter? I bet you don't know how to use a computer–Now that I think about it, my history teacher plays tennis at our club. He asked me to coach his son and I never replied. That kid could use a few tennis pointers from someone who's skilled, practiced, and a natural player."

Elaine Grasshwort smiled beatifically. "And that someone, doubtless, is you. Tennis is a lovely game. So civilized."

Rafe continued to be pleased with himself. "Presto chango. A "B" in history coursework magically is transformed into an "A." And I pick up some change for coaching."

Chapter 8

Big Foot

A full day had gone by since Fred had seen Irie. The horror at finding himself alone in the country house had subsided in Fred. It wasn't entirely gone but it was replaced for the most part with a sad sort of boredom. As he thought about it, he knew that he didn't really want the illusion back again. He still liked trains a lot, but it would have been difficult for Orgone to tempt him again in that way. Fred had gotten older. Still himself, but not quite the same guy. The same bloke, as Irie would say. So he meandered through the rooms and passageways that he found before him, trying windows, seeking an escape route without much confidence that he would succeed. He peered through tall French doors and tried the handles. No success. Outside he could see an English flower garden, full of weeds, with some strikingly colourful flowers peeking through. There was a pond at the bottom of a grassy hill, a hill which had once been covered with a carefully trimmed lawn, but which now was dotted with tall cow parsley. A few ducks were paddling around in the reeds around the pond. In a passageway, he paused to examine a huge foot that had been carved from stone, a piece from a colossus collected long ago by a long-dead, world-traveller owner of the house.

Fred thought to himself in a quiet mood: "The stuff people hauled back from trips to the Mediterranean. Hauled back, back in the day." He smiled to himself. Walking over to the hug stone foot, he gave the toe a tap with his toe. Nothing happened.

Again he thought to himself and almost spoke out loud. "I guess nothing happens unless it's a green toilet that's a cenote. That foot's not going to help me walk out of here." Fred immediately knew he had created a really terrible pun. He produced only a twisty smile at this witticism. But the little language-sin give him a strange, deep pleasure and lifted his mood.

Further down the passageway, he came across an antique chair that had originated in France several hundred years ago. Like the fainting couch it was striped but had gilt legs ending in claws clutching balls. On the chair was a dried cardoon thistle with a long stem. He picked up the thistle and set on the floor. And it was a strange thing, because the house now seemed a little less junk filled and a little more like a museum. They put thistles like that one on chairs in museums to stop you from sitting. By now, he felt more like heritage industry staff than a casual visitor. And, of course, he was sometimes a rebel in small ways so, sat in the forbidden chair, and then settled into it, laying his hands on its arms. "Hum," he thought, and felt a tingle in the fingers of his hands. It was a tingle he had felt before but couldn't remember where.

Looking at the stone foot, Fred wondered to himself: "Where's a bust of Socrates when you need it? I could use some philosophy to lighten things up." Another joke made for his own benefit. But he returned to the dominant theme of his thinking – Where's Irie when you need her? She'd have a plan ready. Or create one so fast it would make your head spin. He lifted the tingling hand and looked under it.

There was a rune just like the rune he had seen on the wooden lychgate support beam in what seemed an eternity ago. Again the rune was the Anglo-Saxon letter "þ," the thorn. He put his hand back down on it and enjoyed the tingling this time. In fact, he felt relaxed by the sensation.

And then, before he drifted off to sleep, he knew he was hungry. He opened his eyes and there, perched on the stone foot was something wrapped in brown baking paper. And on the floor next to the foot was a steaming cup of brown liquid. There was also a two-litre bottle of water, with a torn label that he couldn't make out. He did not need to be told that before him was a focaccia sandwich and a cup of Mexican chocolate. He ate and drank quickly, ravenously. "Voraciously," he thought. "That's what they always say: "Voraciously."" He made his way back to the fainting couch and lay down. Just before he fell asleep, he wondered if Hobgoblin had sent him the sandwich and Lady Yerba the drink. Maybe at the request of Irie.

Chapter 9

Asking for Help

While Fred was on his way to dreamland after his unsuccessful efforts to escape the dusty country house, Hobgoblin stood chopping veggies. The nattily-dressed small creature was standing on his tall stool at the quartz counter, and Irie had positioned herself right behind him, but he didn't seem to hear her. She had tried "hwaethwegu" once again and it had worked this time, allowing her to make her way to the goblin's kitchen. It was almost as if Hobgoblin could change the locks on the entry to the corbelled arch passageway – in accord with his wishes to receive visitors or not. Just what keys Rafe and Grasshwort used when they wanted to enter that same passageway remained unknown to her.

Irie spoke to the back of the busy chef: "I'm about to go and rescue Freddie from a dusty country house. The trains are gone, but he's there alone in there, and I can't even get you to listen to me. I need some advice. I need some information. And, I really want to take along two focaccia sandwiches wrapped in brown baking paper. He will be famished. I'd like to sit and eat with him. Chat and make him feel happy again. I know he's sad now."

Hobgoblin finished his slicing and dicing. He then put the veggies into a reddish liquid in a small saucepan and consulted his cookbook. Now this cookbook was both his because he owned it and because he had written it. He had had it since the early days of the seventeenth century, when he began recording his kitchen experiments in brown oak-gall ink. Grasshwort was his source for galls for many years, but Grasshwort had gotten to be funny-strange of late. So the explanation for Hobgoblin's failure to answer Irie right away was that he had been worrying about heritage ink while he was chopping away with a skill that would have been the envy of above-ground chefs. It was that worry and cogitation which had stalled Irie in her hopes of an answer to her request for information.

Hobgoblin: "What did you just say, young child?" He paused, adjusted his skinny jeans and stroked his goatee. He had begun to remember her query, which he proceeded to answer – in his own way. "Oh, yes. I recall now." Hobgoblin: "You don't need my permission to extract Fred from his predicament. You don't need any information from me. Just go and do it." He thought for a moment and added: "Don't trouble your mind about food. It's not a problem." He didn't bother to explain to her about the scoff that he and Lady Yerba had sent to Fred while that boy was seated in a fancy French chair in front of the large stone foot. So it was that Hobgoblin left Irie in doubt about the facts on which the phrase "don't trouble your mind" was based. She was reassured when she had been told not to worry, but at the same time she didn't much like being asked to go on trust alone. This was an irritating grown-up human thing to do. Don't ask. Just trust. Also a custom among hipster goblins, apparently.

Irie had hoped for detailed instructions on how to get in and out of the dusty country house. These instructions she would have revised and altered in such a way as to fit with a plan that she had already begun developing. The request the sandwiches had been part of the plan and had served two functions. First, her asking for his food served to flatter the little chef, which she hoped would put him in a mood to cough up info. Score zero on that one. Second, she herself would get something good to eat since she really was hungry. Irie rephrased and repeated the request for food, "It's not just Fred. I'm so hungry I could eat two bowls of gungoi and slice of bitter orange tart."

Hobgoblin complied immediately. He ladled out two full bowls and set them on the table where she had sat with Fred. Then he went to the American fridge and sliced a rather large piece of bitter orange tart. Irie took her place at the table and turned her head to watch all of this. Then her eyes fell on a copy of a book lying closed at the far end of the quartz counter. While Hobgoblin had his back turned to her, she briefly stood to get a better look at the volume. On its cover was a photo of Nigella Lawson, who styled herself a "domestic goddess." Irie knew this very standard cookbook from her mother's kitchen. Irie wisely kept this new knowledge to herself. Hobgoblin was undoubtedly a brilliant chef, but he did not get all of his delightful dishes from the pages full of oak-gall ink. Most importantly, he was not likely to enjoy being reminded that he borrowed from human cooks – human cooks who offered themselves to the world with sensuous smiles from the covers of mass-marked books.

Now, the two bowls of gungoi and the tart were quite a bit more than Irie liked to consume at one sitting but consume she did. She wanted to be polite and also had no desire to be turned into whatever variety of English woodland creature that crossed the Hobgoblin's mind when he saw her push back a tart that was only half eaten. She cheerfully said as she finished the last bite of tart, "Oh thank you so much. That was so wonderful. But, please, sir, can you relent and pass along some tips about how to get in and out of the creepy house?" The house, of course, was not all that creepy, but it was dusty and did pose problems with entry and exit.

Hobgoblin knew when he was being flattered, but he also knew that he could not resist a sincere form of flattery. He knew that if Irie had enjoyed the first bowl of gungoi and he fooled himself into thinking that she didn't really mind the second, even though she was feeling stuffed. Likewise, she absolutely loved the first bite of the tart, so he didn't much notice that she was not deriving complete enjoyment from the second. Irie had been seriously faking it and had disliked his delicacies, then Hobgoblin would have turned her into a Gila monster. Woodland creatures were not on his mind nor had they been for a while. Ever since Fred had mentioned Gila monsters, the little chef had wanted to turn someone, anyone into such an animal, if for no other reason than to be able to take a look at this denizen of desert up close. Irie, however, was safe from becoming a reptile to be seen in the Yuma desert and she relieved by what she soon heard the goblin say.

Hobgoblin decided that it would be best if he let Irie in on some of his doings: "Young Mr Gustafson is right now fast asleep on a lovely art nouveau fainting couch, having consumed a delightful sandwich and a cup of very tasty Mexican chocolate. Can you guess who sent this good fare? Lady Yerba, whom you know well, and me, the H Man."

Irie would have preferred it if Hobgoblin had not called himself the H Man. At somewhere in the neighbourhood of 400 years old he was too ancient for that sort of thing. He was also too ancient for the skinny jeans. The goatee was probably OK. It fit, not in an exact way, with the pictures of King Charles II, which she had often seen in history textbooks.

What she said instead was, "Thank you so much, Mr H Man. And I'll thank Lady Yerba when next I see her. But there is that little last detail. How do I get back to the country house? How do I get into it. How do I free Fred? How do we both escape? I have no memory of how we got there the first time. Perhaps you can jog my memory." She thought that she was being exceedingly polite, especially given the gravity of the situation.

Hobgoblin: "Of course you have no memory of finding your way into the country house, because you didn't. I just plunked you down into that dusty place, and then I provided you with a vague memory that you had gotten there on your own. It's pretty easy to convince people that they have done difficult things all on their own, even if they can't remember any of the details. Especially if they can't remember the details. Well, this time you are going to have to get in there on your own. You're going to have to grow up a bit. Take some responsibility."

You may be sure that Irie was ready to wring Hobgoblin's tiny neck. She was absolutely livid. "Grow up? I'll grow up after you've grown bigger, taller, and a whole lot more tactful." What was this coming as it did from a tiny half-hipster creature that probably hadn't been out of his kitchen in 200 years? How he was able to buy his skinny jeans was a mystery to Irie until she realized that he probably used e-commerce, undoubtedly one of the most monopolistic companies. A company that didn't even know the meaning of the word "eco-friendly."

Irie, thank goodness, did not say these words but only thought them and went on to wonder about the Nigella Lawson cookbook. Her mother had complained about misplacing her own copy. But would Hobgoblin actually purloin a copy belonging to an individual human when he could have visited Waterstone's Books in Orchard Square in the middle of the night – picked up a brand-new copy fresh from the printer. Hum, if he did conduct a midnight raid of Waterstone's, then he was not so kitchen-bound as she had thought.

Irie slowly filled her lungs with the pleasant air of her surroundings, cooled her jets, and said in her best mellifluous voice, "Ok, H Man. Freddie and I will work on his rescue by ourselves as a team, but I don't think he and I are not going to do any more cup hunting for you. It's downright dangerous. After he is free, Fred and I will go back to where we came from and become ordinary kids again. We will grow up but in our own good time and not with any push from you."

Unsurprisingly, the little half-hipster had yet another card to play in their game of flattery and refusals. Hobgoblin: "So go back to the world of ordinary people and leave Fred's little sister stuck in her shell? Doesn't seem like a very nice thing to do." Did Hobgoblin know about Irie's mum's favourite word? "Nice." Seemed like he did. Once again, Irie was being asked to be "nice."

Irie was at first very definite and even angry: "Fred doesn't have a little sister." The moment she said this, Irie began to wonder if Hobgoblin might be right. But, then again, maybe the story of the sister was just a dubious card that he had up his sleeve. So she did not correct herself or amend her statement in any way. She just put on her most contrite look.

Hobgoblin did not stop with the story he was telling: "No little sister as far as you know, yes?"

Irie shrugged off her pose of contrition and offered a pleasant rejoinder: "No little sister as far as I know, no!"

She was not quite sure if her answer made a great deal of sense but she did like the sound of her reply. She cocked her head on one side and waited for him to offer a comeback.

And so Hobgoblin said what Irie was beginning to guess: "You don't know about Nora because you have forgotten her. Forgotten Fred's little sister not entirely but mostly. And you've seen her in the last few days. She's there in Lady Yerba's garden, munching the dahlias."

Irie was not about to thank Hobgoblin for this piece of information. Irie: "Munching dahlias? So that's her name? Nora, the kid sister. How old is she? Let's have some details. And am I going to forget about her ten minutes after I finish talking to you? Am I supposed to see to it that she is changed from a perfectly content snail with a beautiful shell back into an obnoxious little girl without – all without any help from you? Try to be nice, yourself. You ought to be ashamed of yourself."

Now she was beginning to sound like her mum. Irie felt slightly guilty about the "obnoxious little girl" part, since she had no idea of what Nora was like. On the other hand, Irie was quite pleased that she brought up the possibility that Nora could have liked being a snail, liked grazing on dahlias, and would not want to return to the world of small children. In the story of Circe, there was a sailor who had been turned into a pig and wanted to remain that way.

Hobgoblin, however, was not the least bit ashamed of himself and was, rather, put into a very good mood by what

Irie had said: "So scoot! Be on your way! Put on your thinking cap and figure a way into the country house. You've dithered your time away much of today, young child. And here's a hint for you, since you have asked for help. No information, but a hint. Sometimes opportunities arise on their own, arise when they are least expected.

When she left the kitchen this time, she was on her best behaviour. She politely said goodbye and said that she hoped she would be with Fred when next she came for a visit. As she made her way to the end of the corbelled-arch passageway, she was actually pretty confident that she would succeed in releasing her friend from the country house. And then she was pleased by the thought that she would succeed in defeating Orgone, who was, she was sure, behind all of this nonsense.

Chapter 10

Girl Talk

So it was that Irie found herself coming into focus in the tall, green gennel, having left the Hobgoblin's kitchen and once again chanted the Anglo-Saxon word for "nothing." But, here, standing alone with nobody to confront, her mood dipped down, and that Anglo-Saxon word seemed sadly fitting given the sad state of her planning. "Nanwiht." There was nothing really to work on at the front of her head. Rather, the plans that she had been making receded into some place in the back of her brain. She did not use the shortcut through the stickery holly bushes and drifted rather than walked along the main path that went by the Q Pit. Grasshwort and Rafe, as might be expected, were not there, and Irie took the opportunity to stop and read a small sign that gave the history of this pit and others like it. A Q Pit, it said, was used for making white charcoal. Sessile oaks were cut down leaving a foot or two of trunk standing, which then produced long, tall shoots. The shoots were taken and burned while green, a technique that produced a kind of charcoal that gave off the high heat important in good the making steel.

Irie finished reading and went back to letting her mind wander. As she stood there, she recalled that steel scythes had been made however-many hundreds of years ago at the Industrial Hamlet on the other side of the road away from where she was in Ireton Wood. She'd never been to the Hamlet but knew that it was home to trip hammers used in forging steel and to grindstones for sharpening blades. All was run by power provided by a water wheel at the foot of a large mill pond. The pond was home to ducks that floated on it in the summer. In cold winters, they scooted along its ice.

Irie found herself walking in the direction of the RC boat pond at Millhouses Park, and arriving there found a lone boy, perhaps ten, standing with his father and controlling a motorized sail boat. That might have been Freddie six years ago. Not really able to help herself, she made her way to the bench that she shared so often with Fred. Their special place where the could talk frankly about families and friends and lots and lots of things. The atmosphere was empty without Fred. "Buggah," she said to herself. "Buggah, buggah, buggah." It felt good to say that word. Not quite a "bad" word but not a good one either. Perfect for a bleak mood.

Irie, sitting on the bench away from the orange lichen, opened the mutual backpack, taking out the mahogany box. As she was allowing her eyes to pass over the armorial crest that and the inscription MIR, a very light-haired girl, wearing pale make-up and dressed in a pleasant white summer dress slowly sailed by as if she were a boat on the pond. But a boat not controlled by anyone other than herself. After walking on some distance, the girl turned and sailed back towards Irie. Irie knew her by sight. A girl from High Storrs School.

Without asking, the girl sat at the other end of the bench from Irie and said as sweetly as a girl could say, "Oooh! That's a pretty box. Can I look at it?"

Irie instinctively told a lie. It was a good lie, a wise lie, a lie that made perfect sense under the circumstances. Irie drew the box closer to her chest. "I'm sorry. This is a family heirloom and my mother would kill me if it were scratched or anything. It came all the way from Canada. My gran brought it here and gave it to me today because it's my birthday."

Now it might be argued that Irie could have accomplished her purpose of deflecting the girl's request with something less than the full-throated lie that included a mythical grandmother from Canada and a non-existent birthday. But the grandmother and the birthday did give Irie both a certain satisfaction and renewed energy. It eased her own becalmed purpose out of the doldrums, in which it had been languishing like the boat from "Rhyme of the Ancient Mariner," a set text from English class.

The girl in white did not relent. "Oh, I won't scratch it. I'll handle it gently. Kid gloves. That sort of thing."

Irie would not have been surprised if the girl were in fact wearing white kid gloves, but this was only an old expression. And who had ever really seen kid gloves.

Maybe Hobgoblin when he was first getting started writing his brown gall ink cookbook.

Irie felt but did not show irritation. She was definite: "No, really. Do I know you?" Irie, of course, did know the girl as someone who was at school, but it was enjoyable to talk down in a pleasant, polite way."

The girl continued to press the matter, "Sure you do. I'm three years above you and Fred. Year 14. And I'm Florimell. My mother found the name in a book. An old one. The book." Now this was strange business. Florimell knew Fred or knew about Fred. Irie found herself being drawn into the conversation, even if she also felt a temptation to correct the girl about "above." It really should be "older." And then Irie thought to herself that not many at High Storrs did the extra year, the year that would help them towards admission at this or that university. Year 14. This was definitely an older girl. Experienced and not in good ways, apparently.

Irie: "What a pretty name. So, you know Fred Gustafson? Shall I call you Flora? And the extra year at High Storrs really does make you very full of knowledge. What are your plans for university?"

Florimell: "Of course I know Fred. I came down to the boat pond today to see if I could find him. I haven't seen him around in the last day or two. And, no, I never shorten my name. Just Florimell. That's what people call me."

Irie became suspicious and abruptly observed: "I've never seen you here." Irie was not going to like what she was to hear next from Florimell.

Florimell: "That's because we usually go to the Industrial Hamlet. Freddie loves the water wheel and the grindstones and all the belts that drive the grindstones, making them go round and round." Once again, Irie wanted to wring someone's neck, and this time it wasn't Hobgoblin's.

Before she could stop herself, Irie lost her cool and abruptly asked in a threatening voice, "You go with Fred to the Industrial Hamlet?"

Florimell: "Yeah, we get hot chocolate at the cafe, and we watch the men forge bottle openers at the fiery hearths next to the grindstones. Fred is really into history, but I guess you already know that. They used to make scythe blades at the Hamlet. Years ago. It's just a museum now."

As Irie began to regain her mental composure, she decided to probe this story of a friendship between Fred and Florimell. Irie: "I once suggested the Industrial Hamlet to Fredrick and he said that he didn't like that sort of stuff." This was an out and out lie, but Irie wanted to see how Florimell would reply. Irie was not pleased with the answer she received.

Florimell: "I shouldn't say this and don't tell anyone, but it's sort of 'our place.' You know, me and Freddie. Just for us." Now, this little bit of secret information imparted by Florimell again enraged Irie, though Irie was buoyed up by the thought that Florimell was matching her own earlier lie with a bigger whopper.

Irie's voice was full of condescension: "Frederick has never mentioned you. Absolutely never said a word."

Florimell smiled sympathetically. "He wouldn't, would he? After all, he's an American. You know, over-paid and over here. The other thing."

Irie felt just a little relief. If Florimell was trying to wind her up, Irie was not going to let that happen. And Fred. "Oversexed," the other thing that Florimell had suggested, did not really fit this boy. "I simply do not believe you. Freddie Gustafson is not that kind of boy." Irie felt like a girl in an American movie of the 1930s and 40s. Maybe Dorothy confronting the Wicked Witch of the West. Irie was putting on an act, but she enjoyed what she was doing.

Florimell: "Not that kind of boy. As far as you know. Yes?"

Irie almost burst out laughing. She found herself having a version of the conversation that she had had with Hobgoblin about Nora. Irie: "As far as I know. No." Irie was not agreeing with Florimell and Florimell knew it.

Nevertheless, Florimell persisted. Florimell: "I am not here to convince you. That, and we are definitely not boy and girl friend, if that's what has you worried. He's got some ways to go before that sort of relationship could develop. Just a kid. Crushes. Puppy love." Irie immediately understood this statement from Florimell as a filthy, lousy, disgusting lie. That understanding gave Irie some relief from discussing a topic so sensitive.

With the statement about puppy love still hanging in the air, Florimell stood and sailed away back down towards the RC boat pond. Irie was suddenly struck by something. Florimell had been sitting on the orange lichen, but her light, white summer frock had collected not a whit of orange stain. What was going on here? And how could Florimell remember Freddie when Hobgoblin said that even his family wouldn't remember as long as he was prisoner of the dusty country house. And yet, for all of her lies, there could be some truth in what Florimell said. Maybe there were meetings at the Industrial Hamlet coffee shop. Meetings that were innocent on Fred's part but not so innocent on the part of Florimell. Maybe the girl in white was leading him on. What had Fred told her about Morgan le Fey and King Arthur? She wished she could remember.

Chapter 11

Grindstones

There was deafening noise as Fred and Florimell looked at the row of spinning grindstones, power transferred by leather belts from a water wheel outside. This was one of the days that the Industrial Hamlet was both open for visitors and running its very old machinery, machinery dating back hundreds of years. There needed to be updates for safety and replacement parts for wear and tear, of course, But the "experience," as heritage professionals put it, was authentic. Certainly the experience was authentic where the noise level was concerned.

Florimell spoke over the roar of the machinery: "Let's get out of here, too noisy."

Fred: "I can't hear you, Florimell." She smiled and gently pulled him towards the door by the sleeve of his Yuma Criminals tee. When they were outside, she continued.

Florimell: "You know you should lose that tee. The guy on it looks like something out of a 1950s comic book."

Fred: "The Arizona Territorial Penitentiary figures in a big way in the history of Yuma, Yuma where I was born and lived until I was unwillingly dragged here by my otherwise loving parents. Kids at Yuma High decided to have as their mascot a tough guy from the prison. Other schools have mountain lions, or wolves, or rattlesnakes. Our mascot is this criminal." Fred chanted the chant from football games. (American football, of course.)

"We are the criminals. And couldn't be prouder.

If you can't hear us now, we'll yell a little louder."

Florimell still thought the tee a fashion disaster, but she remained her pleasant self. Or, at least, did a good job of seeming pleasant.

Florimell: "Let's go to the coffee shop and get some of that sweet hot chocolate that you like so much." And that's exactly what they did. They walked away from the grindstone room and up a little hill, going by a huge trip hammer, and to the modern, well-appointed coffee shop.

Florimell and Fred took a table next to a window that gave a fine view of the industrial part of the hamlet. The workers houses, restored to 19th century furniture and other appointments, were on the other side of the cafe. Fred had ordered the hot chocolate and she and asked for a skinny latte. As the drinks were being made, she asked him about his family.

Florimell: "Who are your people? Who do you come from? But first let me tell you about me. My mum's Malory. We're not from Wales, but she loves Welsh history and likes to read romance novels. I think she might be secretly collecting stories for some sort of book. I'm an only child. What about you?"

Fred was taken off guard and he did not really want to talk about his family. He was especially reluctant to say anything about his mother. He was about to say that his sister, Melanie was stuck on Rafe, but then stopped. And then there was the nagging feeling that his father wasn't the only remaining member of the family. Fred just sat there and looked flummoxed.

Florimell rescued the situation by saying how impressed she was with all of the machinery they had just seen. He brightened up and became filled with boyish enthusiasm. Fred: "Talk about nose to the grindstone."

Florimell played along: "What an image. I can certainly imagine." She let her voice trail off so that he could continue to enthuse.

Fred: "Yeah, guys sharpening scythes on those grindstones. I wonder what they used to protect their eyes. And the leather belts. What a set up." Then the drinks came. As the cafe staff began to put down the blue and white cups, Florimell, reaching for hers, accidentally brushed the back of Fred's hand with the tip of her little finger. He moved his hot chocolate closer to himself and wondered if he should apologize. Then he got a funny little smile on his face and dismissed that piece of politeness. She offered him a paper packet of sugar to add to his chocolate. He thought about whether he wanted it.

***

Irie was still sitting on the bench under the sessile oak, and Florimell was long gone now. Their bench. Hers and Freddie's. She was talking to herself. Maybe she had nodded off. Maybe had been dreaming again, if it was a dream and not something else. She avoided tearing up, but was on the edge. She spoke very quietly in a hushed voice: "Don't let your imagination run away with itself." And then she wiped her face with the back of her hand.

PART THREE

Chapter 1

Dumbwaiter

It was morning and the day after Fred had parted ways with Irie. He had slept pretty well on the lovely art nouveau fainting couch (as Hobgoblin had described it) and was now meandering without much purpose down a long passageway. He had almost given up hope of escape. On both walls of the passageway, there were groups of family photographs separated by a series of windows. Out of one of the windows he again saw the weedy garden, which had become a little tidier. The duck pond at the bottom of the lawn was no longer choked with reeds. Indeed, the lawn had become more civilized. He thought to himself: "There are little piles of sheep poo out there. They look like little black marbles. Somebody must graze sheep on a regular basis. It does save fuel for lawnmowers and probably fertilizes the grass." He walked on down the passageway until another thought struck him: "On the other hand, you need to watch where you step." He examined the photos, which included many in black and white of men in celluloid collars and of women wearing dresses with high collars and bustles. There was a scattering of little boys in sailor suits and girls in white dresses. A good thing that that the sailor suit fashion had disappeared. He would not like to know that somewhere there were photos of himself in such a getup. He thought of the song in Sound of Music about girls in white dresses. That thought made him feel strange. Both happy and frightened. He wondered why.

The passageway led on to a large, well-equipped, 1880s kitchen, which had been built away from the main house so that the owners would not be bothered by the smells of cooking. The kitchen had pipes hanging from the ceiling that would have provided gas for lighting at some point long ago. Fred tried the windows again. No luck.

He poked around, opening dusty cupboards. He tried the tap on the sink and out came yellowish-brown water. This made him thirsty, and even though he knew he would never drink the stuff unless he was desperate, he opened more cupboards looking for a drinking glass. In one of the dustiest, he found a fresh focaccia sandwich on plate that was covered with cling film. No dust on the cling film.

Next to the sandwich was another plate with, again under cling film, a bitter orange tart. Finally there was a two-litre plastic bottle of water on which was a paper label that read: "Purveyors of Still and Sparkling Water to HM Q Mab." The food and drink was hugely welcome, and he drank deeply of the water first. Equally welcome because of the fact that somebody was looking after him as he worked on finding a way out. Or maybe he was just being given a little to eat and drink as he waited for Irie to rescue him. In any event, Fred stood while he ate and drank at a tall pinewood table that had seen heavy use over the years. It was a place where kitchen staff did their work.

And then he noticed that the table was actually clean. No dust. It had just been rubbed down with a wet cloth recently, and for some reason this fact was not spooky at all. More of a reassurance. With the last of his sandwich in hand, he continued to open cabinet doors until he came across a dumbwaiter hidden behind a very large one. The dumbwaiter was composed of wooden platform suspended on a rope with a counterweight. The device had a crank so it could be wound up and down. The platform was large enough for him to sit on, and so he did, saying to himself: "I wonder if . . ."

Working the rope with his hands, Fred let himself down into the room below. You didn't have to use the crank if you sat on the platform. Once down to the lower level, he climbed out, and, while looking around, saw against the opposite wall a food-transport tunnel, once used to convey meals from the odorous kitchen to the sweet-smelling main house. On the floor of the tunnel were two steel railway tracks on which a large trolley ran. The trolley was blocking the entrance to the tunnel and, without giving the matter much consideration, Fred rolled it back. Like the baby buggy in the room where he found the box of trains, the axels on the trolley were rusty, but not so rusty as to keep the wheels from turning.

Fred thought to himself almost out loud: "This just might be a way out of here. At the other end of the tunnel should be another dumbwaiter that will be connected to the main dining room above. I've been through the whole house, and I've yet to see a dining room. Maybe there are large French doors connected to the patio. Maybe this is all a game and I escape if I'll take a few risks. If Irie were here, what would she tell me to do?"

And then he entered the tunnel: "My god this place is cold and damp, but in for a dime, in for a dollar." And so he went forward in the semi-darkness. In point of fact the tunnel was not far underground and had widows at regular intervals at the tops of the walls. While the windows were filthy and covered with tall grass in places, they gave enough light so that Fred could see pretty well what was ahead of him. As he moved along, taking care not to catch his feet or cut his hands, his mood improved hugely. He was developing a new sense of adventure. Hope was in there too, and it was good to be pursuing a possible avenue of possible escape.

**

While Fred was making his way down the food-trolley tunnel, Irie spent the morning at her desk tapping away at a computer. She had been avoiding what she was about to do. She was just a bit frightened of what she might see on the screen in front of her. But she went ahead and brought up "Orgone." She read the Wikipedia entry, and followed the followed a link to Wilhelm Reich. She continued browsing through other web pages, some of which were difficult to understand or just downright "random," as Fred would have said had been sitting next to her. Though he wasn't, she did feel better about him than she did when she finished talking with Florimell. But Florimell presented another problem. Irie was not quite sure if she had really had the conversation with this girl in white or if she had dreamed it. Imagined it. Had it crept into her imaginary through some sort of back door. Well, the person who would know was likely to be Lady Yerba, though this very wise Latina woman could not be relied upon to say all she knew. So, what you do in a case like this, Irie understood very well, is to drop a few suggestive statements and see what response will come back to you. No direct questions.

Iric made her way to Lady Yerba's house, lingering for a moment on the red-pillar post box. That boy would be swinging around it if he were with her. She moved along quickly, making her way up the driveway, and giving a quick tap to the cenote with her Converse trainer. Fred would have said "sneaker." Lady Yerba beamed a lovely white smile at her and pointed at the second chair, the one that was always there. Irie sat, and then saw a small bowl of menudo sitting on the bottom of a large upside-down flowerpot. The pot was brightly painted with tropical birds and beside it was a very old spoon. The bowl was clearly intended for her. It was warm. Lady Yerba knew she was coming. Irie looked at the back of the spoon and found its hallmark. Made in Sheffield. The spoon was old enough to have been buffed by a buffer girl in the 1880s.

Irie began, "What a lovely spoon. Sheffield and a little Mexican stew. Just the right amount. I wonder if Freddie found anything to eat and drink. Now that the illusion is gone, he is sure to be hungry."

Lady Yerba began, "We sent him something yesterday and then again today. Something that I think he'll like." She didn't say who the "we" was and Irie calculated that it might be best not to ask, but rather to let Lady Yerba keep on talking. "The young gentleman was quite hungry this morning and probably would not have been choosy about what he found in the kitchen cupboard, but we tried to present him with something nice. There was the food and the good thoughts that go with food. He is happier."

There it was, that word again. "Nice." But rather than comment on the similarity between Lady Yerba and her mother, Irie said, "I'm so glad that Freddie has had a bit of food to fill his tummy. He gets cranky when he isn't properly fed. With a little food, with a little energy, he is sure to make his way out of that dusty stately home and back to us. Oh, maybe back to his family first."

Lady Yerba was perfectly well aware that Irie wanted a clear suggestion, a direct course of action in which Irie would be the rescuer. But Lady Yerba had no intention supplying this information. Rather she spoke carefully in a measured tone: "You will be crucial in the young man's escape from Orgone. But this is less a matter of your mapping out a plan and more a case of keeping your eyes and ears open. Watching for the signs, and making the right move when opportunity presents itself. And then there is emotion. You will feel it strongly but don't let it make you 'tonta'.

Irie stared at this woman sitting across from her and offered a blank look.

Lady Yerba: "I apologize, I said "silly" or a "fool." That's tonta. You are neither silly nor a fool. But that is the bad temptation." Irie understood perfectly and was pleased to have the warning. Irie was less pleased by what followed, for Lady Yerba went on to say, "Like the young man, you will have to deal with Orgone. This is dangerous." Then Lady Yerba shifted her serious tone and once again beamed with a smile: "But I have faith in you, hija. You will not fail."

Irie for a moment wanted to "accidentally" drop the bowl of menudo on the floor. Splash it on the feet of the woman who gave advice that was not advice. No hint of ideas for a practical plan. Only, a stern warning in the most vague terms. And then this bit about "Go get 'em, girl," from a spectator. If this woman was some sort of good bruja from a movie about a girl from Kansas, why didn't she just wave a magic wand transport Freddie onto the driveway in front of them? Why did she have to be so effing confident that it was all going to be OK. "Effing." A far more "appropriate" word right now than "nice."

Chapter 2

Sharpening Scythe Blades

Fred didn't cut his fingers on the walls of the kitchen tunnel, but he did feel spots that were slimy, probably from algae or moss. And it was a good thing that kept first this and then that hand on the wall's surface, because he suddenly stumbled and caught himself before he fell. Stopping to look at what had snagged his foot, he discovered piece of food-trolley rail that had come loose from the floor and was now sticking straight up. And then finally after however many yards of tunnel, he began to see light. He resisted the urge to speed up his pace. He was well aware that there would be more foot catchers ahead. And he was right. Just before he emerged into a large room, he found a metal tray smack in the centre of his path, positioned over both of the trolley rails. Had he stepped on it, he would have gone flying. It is difficult to imagine just how much satisfaction avoiding that little trap gave to him, Maybe not a trap, but a tray left by a careless kitchen servant how many years ago? The 1880s? Why did that decade jump into his brain? He had little time to ponder this question as he was immediately hit with unexpected news.

Rather than being a food-service area below a dining room, it was an industrial storage room, complete with stacks of rusty scythe blades piled haphazardly on shelves. Arranged in rows along one wall were grindstones large and small. There was no dumbwaiter to be seen, only a narrow wooden staircase leading to the floor above. In his haste to examine the shelves, he didn't notice the staircase. On a deep long shelf, there were lengthy leather bands of the sort used to transfer power from a central set of spinning wheels to pulleys in some kind of manufacturing sctup. Fred had seen the lace-making machines of 150 years ago at a museum in Nottingham. But this was not a weaving mill. Then he twigged. Which is to say that he knew that Irie would tell him that he "twigged." Strange how other people's words jump into your head. But twigged it was at first and then, trailing along afterwards in his brain was "light bulb moment." This storage area had to be under the Industrial Hamlet. Yes, the Industrial Hamlet across the road from Ireton Wood.

Fred began to talk to himself out loud, though completely unaware that he was holding this conversation while alone. And maybe he was talking to Irie, not quite remembering that she wasn't present.

Fred: "They imported the steel in bulk from Sweden. Made the blades. Attached the blades to Sheffield steel shafts. Used the grindstones to sharpen the blades. And mounted the finished shaft and blade to wooden handles."

Then he caught himself talking in a serious voice: "Buggah." He said it but for a second he thought it was her. Irie talking. Again, he was strangely happy and a further thought increased his pleasure. If he was not under a country house dining room. Instead he was under the grindstone room at the Industrial Hamlet Museum.

And he said to himself: "Out. I'm out of the stinking, low-down, lying, enchanted country house. Out into a world where you could walk in the sunshine. Watch RC boats on a pond once again. Eat little chocolate frogs."

And then Fred became immersed in doing a close examination of what was on the shelves. The scythes, the leather bands, the nuts and bolts. Heavy steel hammers. He began to sharpen one of the rusty scythes on a grindstone that was propped up against a wall.

***

While Fred was thus engaged, Irie was getting herself a second bowl of menudo in Lady Yerba's kitchen. Irie sunk a long-handled ladle deep into the savory fluid of a black, cast-iron pot. The herbs and spices along with whatever other ingredients in there smelled deliriously inviting, strangely inviting in fact. She felt herself overcome with emotion she had never experienced before and couldn't describe. She didn't want to drop into a faint there on the kitchen floor, so she put her bowl on the counter, left the ladle sunk in the pot, and in a wobbly movement took a chair at the kitchen table. Without even thinking about it further, she put her head on the tabletop and went to sleep. Or maybe that's what it was.

***

Now years later, a thirty-something woman with kids at Totley Elementary School down south quite a ways from Millhouses Park, Irie isn't quite sure if she dreamed an exotic dream or saw something akin to the visions sent to mystics and lunatics. In either case, what happened was seared in her memory. The rational, sensible person in her thinks in terms of psychology and says that this was just a vivid anxiety dream. That she was completely exhausted from trying to come up with rescue plans, and her fears welled up from her subconscious as she slept at Lady Yerba's kitchen table. Her children's grandmother often said, "Stress shows itself in strange ways."

The other more canny person in Irie is pretty certain that the first bowl of menudo and the deep aroma of the second were directly involved in what happened when her head was resting on the table. The food and the food smell triggered something. Irie knows that lots of menudo sits atop stoves in Mexico, but she is also well aware that not every Latina cook includes in the recipe all the ingredients that Lady Yerba favors. Yes, what about those roots that Irie had gathered for the Mexicana with the green toilet bowl? Irie remembered that in her naive trust in Lady Yerba back then she had enthusiastically dug roots from the rich black soil of a secret place. Irie had marvelled at the red highlights. She had been fascinated with the sprouting orange hairs. Now, these many years later, Irie suspects that Lady Yerba used the vegetable that came from beneath that fertile soil to create a vision. To create Irie's vision. Irie remembered seeing the ugly/beautiful thing lying there on the kitchen counter before she put her head down on the table. Seeing the root so many years ago on the on the drain board, reminds her now of the ginger that her mother often used. But it wasn't ginger that was in Lady Yerba's kitchen. That was for sure.

***

After she was awake again and sitting still a little bleary-eyed in the kitchen, Irie asked Lady Yerba about the smell of the menudo. The reply that came back specified chayote. But this was not chayote. The kindly old bruja, if that was what she was, didn't give up her secrets that easily.

The dream itself (or maybe vision) was set in the Industrial Hamlet. Irie saw herself looking down at Fred from a raised platform high above him. From this, this supervisor's station, she could see that he had his nose almost literally touching a spinning grindstone. The grindstone, connected to a power source above by a long leather belt, was turning at medium speed in front of him. He was dressed in a tweed jacket as if it were 1880 and was wearing a flat cap backwards. He had no protective glasses and the scythe blade he was sharpening spewed out sparks, sparks falling in a broad arc in front of him. It might have been Fourth of July fireworks. For a moment she stopped and wondered, why fourth of July and not Guy Fawks night? The thought disappeared as quickly as it came, and Irie decided to make her way down the steps from the platform above. If she didn't stop the sharpening, then a spark was sure to bounce off of something and fly into one of his eyes. But Irie's limbs were weary and she leaned heavily against the platform's railing. Her hands were numb. All she could do was watch.

Florimell had arranged herself in the stance of shop foreman,. Almost a man rather than a woman. She, like Fred, was dressed as if it were somewhere in the 1880s. She wore riding pants but her white shirt was loose and billowing out from her arms. On this account, she looked a little like a female version of the male character Poldark from Irie's favourite TV show about pirates. Florimell wore English riding boots and held a clipboard that had a piece of paper on it. With a quill pen, she was ticking off boxes.

As if in a movie close-up, Irie could see that the paper was for marking dressage scores. At least that was what it said in large letters at the top. And Fred's score? Fred was not doing well. His top number was five and his lowest was zero. For a second or two, Irie thought to herself, that she was in a dream and that she must wake herself. She shuddered and shook, but the scene did not change. Freddie continued to sharpen the scythe blade and continued to take chances with his vision as the sparks radiated out in front of him.

Florimell spoke, "You love machines, don't you? Are you close enough to one now?"

Irie expected to see a fiendish smile emerge on Florimell's face, but Florimell actually seemed bored. Or maybe Florimell was just pretending. Fred sat up from his work and turned to confront Florimell with a mix of indignation and disgust: "I've been at this for more than an hour. I want a tea break. You have to give it me. It's the law, innit?"

Now Florimell's interest was raised: "Banging on at me about workers' rights, are ye. Health and safety. Child labour laws. And since when did Americans ever want a tea break? Maybe a cup of hot chocolate if you can find one. A little paper packet of sugar to add? But I think all you really want is a chance to get back behind the bicycle shed and have a smoke. I've seen the stains on your fingers. You must roll your own."

Suddenly another close-up appeared to Irie and she saw a hand yellowed with nicotine and tar. And then she thought, it's a hand with yellow fingers, but is it Fred's? I've got to change this story that I am in. Or maybe, just maybe, I need to stay in it. Need to use it. Make this story work for me."

Florimell: "You've sharpened only three blades in the last hour and done a sad job of it. Once you learn to do the work properly, you shall have a brief respite. High Storrs

School history classes are all for the children of wealthy parents. And yourin ain't."

Fred stood and raised his arm with the scythe's glinting blade held high above his head. He brought the beautiful piece of Swedish steel down onto a block of wood, where it stuck firmly. Then he turned and glowered at Florimell: "You worthless posho, you upper-class CHAV. I don't want a tea break. I don't want a cup of chocolate with extra sugar in it. I want to see my friends. My mom. My big sister. And I want to see Irie. Yes Irie."

Florimell was delighted. Now here was a little interest. Not the passive, mardi bum who had been quietly bent over sharpening scythe blades until his back ached like the victim of an Anglo-Saxon curse. "Erce, Erce," she said to herself starting just such a curse, but then she stopped herself and said: "You'd like to collect your pennies and go off to the pub. You'd love to get stinking drunk with that filthy little Irie. You have a loving wife Flora at home along with your two adorable children. Instead of being with them, you spend your time with the tiny slut. And what about your little sister? What about little Nora Gustafson? Have you forgotten her?"

Fred simply did not know how to respond to the horrible word that Florimell had used to insult Irie. People don't talk like that in real life. Not people he knew. Or maybe they did and he chose to forget it. So he responded to Florimell's mysterious accusation of forgetfulness, "I don't have a little sister. I have a big sister, the math boffin. Irie has a little brother. Sanka. It's Irie you're thinking about. We hid from Irie's mum under the lychgate, to get away from Sanka. Nice kid, though."

Irie didn't know whether to explode at the word "nice" or to feel relief that she was suddenly there watching Fred.

Florimell: "You have no little sister? None that you know of. That doesn't mean none at all."

Fred who had been wearing heavy leather shoes with wooden soles, took one off and shoved it into space between the grindstone and its wooden frame. The stone came to a scrunching halt. The belt jumped off if its pulley and fell to the floor with a slap. Fred was pleased with himself. Irie was even more pleased. Fred looked at Florimell and said as if making a joke between them, "You can take this job and . . ."

Florimell, for whatever reason, was also pleased. She sang out in her best Johnny Paycheck voice: "Take this job and shove it. I ain't workin' here no more." Florimell continued the song: "Has your 'woman done left you?' Did Irie leave you to find your way out of the stinking, low-down, country house on your own?" Florimell enjoyed the parody of Fred's words for the country house.

Fred: "Yeah, that's some of the words to the song. But I think you have a problem here with your equipment. You'll need to call the maintenance people to put the belt back on the grindstone. Or maybe they've decided to go on strike. As for me, I'm taking a permanent break." Fred strode towards the door.

Florimell was delighted with what she was about to say: "But you can't go until I say so, because of what you did to me. Do you want me to tell everyone what you did to me? Tell Irie?"

Irie was outraged. She pointed her finger at the vile year 13 girl, the girl in the billowy white pirate top and yelled out: "You, whoever you are. Stop. Stop right now. He didn't do anything to you."

But she couldn't hear herself. She yelled but there was no sound. She was sure she was dreaming, sure but she couldn't change the rules of the dream. And maybe it wasn't a dream. Maybe she was experiencing hallucinations. Maybe something else. She wanted to get back to reality, but knew she had to endure what this horrible woman would go on to say. Endure it. Live thorough it. Disbelieve it. Half believe it. And then Irie knew who she was. This human girl, or whatever she was, was Florimell who refused be called Flora because of a sister with that name. The girl on the bench whose white frock was not discoloured by sitting on orange algae.

Fred: "It was only a cup of hot chocolate. That's all." All at once, Irie found the whole situation terribly comic. Fred had shared a table with Florimell and had a cup of hot chocolate. He should have told her. Sure. But gimme a break. This was not the London gold heist. Not the crime of the century.

Florimell went on, "But you touched my hand. That touching my hand makes you my beau. HA! Beau, you? You can sharpen a few scythes or? Would you like to be a sparrow scouting for focaccia crumbs? Or maybe a hoddy dod scooting along on a glistening trail of slime and eating dahlias?"

Before she knew it was happening, Irie found her voice. She heard herself speaking. Saw Florimell and Fred both turn and look. Both listen to her words.

Irie: "You horrible woman, Florimell. You put something into that hot chocolate. He doesn't like you and never will. You can take your white face powder and your fake riding boots, and you know what you can do with them."

Chapter 3

A Visit to the Industrial Hamlet Cafe

Irie was talking loudly as she sat with her head down on the table in the kitchen, and Lady Yerba decided that it was time to bring the girl back into this world by gently nudging a shoulder. As Irie lifted her head, she could feel her heart pounding. Gradually it slowed and her breathing became normal. Pleased, Lady Yerba turned her attention to the kitchen sink, where she busied herself filling a glass with water from the tap. Irie, still sitting, turned to accept the water and smiled a faint smile. Gradually, Irie began to go over in her mind what was happening. What to say to Lady Yerba? What to just let pass? And what did Lady Yerba know anyway? Maybe Lady Yerba was totally clued up. No need to spill the horror of it all to the bruja who knew the story already. The "nice" bruja. And so the two of then, the older woman and Irie, who felt much younger than she really was, left the kitchen and took their appointed places in the aluminium chairs on the porch.

Lady Yerba: "Irie, you were far, far away. Maybe fainted. Something. And you were talking muy rudiosa. Very loud. I had to wake you up."

Irie continued to return to normal: "Thanks for the water. And for the menudo." Irie had her suspicions about that tasty bowl of soup but kept them to herself.

Lady Yerba: "Denada, hija." Irie had picked up a little Spanish one summer on holiday in Alacante. She remembered that "hija" meant daughter and wondered if Lady Yerba thought of her in that way. A daughter." Irie felt a sudden urge to be about her own business. She needed to execute a plan that was quickly forming in her brain.

Irie: "But, I gotta go."

Lady Yerba: "Where so quickly?"

Irie: "Not the country house. Not to where the trains are. Where the trains were. Now gone. I'm not going there. I have an idea. If it works, I'll tell you."

And with that brief leave-taking, Irie rose and shot like an arrow down the driveway. Lady Yerba thought to herself: "When that girl gets an idea, it turns into a plan in the blink of her deep brown eye."

***

Irie opened the door to the Industrial Hamlet coffee shop and marched up to the counter. Not bothering with such Sheffield pleasantries as "hiya," she pointedly asked the middle-aged woman looking at receipts in the cash register: "Have you seen a boy about my age? Today? I think he was wearing – I can't remember." The woman at first did not look up and or respond. Then she presented a pleasant smile and said: "No boys your age in here today, love." This response made Irie giggle, because Freddie could never get used to the idea that in Sheffield women in the shops called everyone "love." Freddie knew that these were not pervies, and he knew that if he were in Nottingham they'd call you "dook." He would have liked that better, he said, being a "duck." And then he began on the rhyme from his youth which ran contrary to what he had just said.

I don't wanna be a chicken I don't wanna be a duck

I just want to dance around and shake my butt.

Irie was never amused by this rhyme, but that did not stop Fred from repeating it. And then she remembered that he was wearing that Yuma tee.

Irie scanned the room and saw a girl sitting at one of the bistro tables. This girl had the same facial features as Florimell and the same sort of body, but her skin was not so fair and her hair was auburn rather than blond. The girl was dressed in blue jeans and had on a blue Hard Rock Cafe tee. She was wearing no makeup. Irie was momentarily flummoxed. She didn't know what to do, but that moment did not last. So, she strode up to the girl's table and asked to sit down. There were many unoccupied tables so this was a bold move, but Irie was feeling bold. The girl in the jeans and the Hard Rock tee smiled a neutral sort of smile. She was almost welcoming, but not warmly.

Irie: "Have you seen Fred today? Maybe not in here in the coffee shop but around the Industrial Hamlet? Over in Ireton Wood?"

171

The girl continued neutral in attitude: "Do I know you?"

Irie: "From High Storrs School."

The girl: "Oh, yes. I think I recall. You're some years below me."

Irie: "Yeah, same year as Fred Gustafson. I'm pretty sure you've noticed Fred around school. He likes history. Talks a lot."

The girl: "Oh yeah. I saw him in here a couple of weeks ago. The place was packed. Nowhere to sit, so he asked if he could have a chair at my table."

Irie: "And you said 'yes.'"

The girl: "Sure, why not? He wasn't the least bit weird. Nice kid. Likes history. . . Oh. I heard you say that. Were you supposed to meet him here?"

Irie decided to lie. Indeed, she enjoyed the lie even as she told it. Savoured it: "Yes. About twenty minutes ago. I was waiting outside to walk in with him. I guess he's just late."

The girl: "Men of all ages. Men in all ages. Stone age to now. All late. Mansplaining, Manspreading. Late."

Irie was not one to casually trash boys to other girls, but continued her interrogation without letting up: "So that was the only time you ever saw him here at the Industrial Hamlet?"

The girl was not put off by the pointed questions but thought she would probe a little herself: "What are you getting at?"

Irie: "I mean, have you seen him around the Industrial Hamlet today?"

The girl: "No, but he might be down at the grindstone sharpening room. It's running now. Belts whizzing and whirring. Some days it's still. Today, pretty loud."

Irie was thrown off balance with emotion: "Grindstones sharpening scythe blades? Today?"

The girl: "Yeah. You can see the building out of the window. Just down there." The girl in the blue jeans and the blue Hard Rock Cafe tee stood up a little, turned halfway and looked down towards the buildings at the bottom of a cobblestone drive.

Irie: "I gotta get going." She rose and ambled to the door with nonchalance that was completely unconvincing. She knew it. The girl knew it. That was one of the few things the two of them had in common.

The girl. "Ta, see you round school." The girl didn't really talk like a person who would say "ta" for "bye" and, again, both knew what was happening. The girl was pretending to "be" Sheffield.

After Irie had left, the girl rose and asked the lady at the counter for the restroom. The loo. And as an aside, said to the counter lady, "Irie keeps that boy on a short chain. Or tries to."

The counter lady simply said, "Toilet over there," and did not look up, but nodded in the direction of the needed facility.

***

173

The girl was wrong or had intentionally misled Irie for the ancient machinery was not running. This, of course, was a huge relief for Irie who vividly recalled this same room with Fred positioned at the sharpening seat, nose to the whirring grindstone. Now, the stone was still. The belts were still, too, but firmly attached. And the grindstone could turn freely because there was no leather shoe with a wooden sole stuck between it and the frame. Just as she was about to heave a sigh of relief, Irie saw that, although the stone was free to turn, the shoe in question was sitting on the floor beside it. The wooden sole of the shoe was cracked down the middle. This was not a shoe that anyone could wear again.

But there were no museum visitors in the grindstone room and most definitely no Fred to be seen. First frightened, then relieved, and then disappointed, Irie turned to leave and took a few steps. She stopped because she heard something. Perhaps an animal rustling around in the room below. She was able to see into that room through an opening in the floor but it was just a place to store junk. Well, if not junk then old grindstone machinery parts.

Again there was the noise. Clinking of some sort and after that a definite word in English: "Buggah." And the voice. Could it be? Irie moved her position this way and that as she peered down through an opening in the floor. The room was dimly lit, and she couldn't see well. But she knew the voice. Yes, it was Fred's and then she made out what he was doing. He was assembling a scythe. He pushed a shaft of Sheffield steel into a hole in a long wooden handle, a shaft topped with fine steel from Sweden. Rusty but fine steel. He pushed and twisted at the same time. Once again, he uttered the maybe-bad word, "Buggah."

Irie: "Fredrick Gustafson, put that thing down right now. Now! I mean now. You're going to cut off a finger, and I'll have to take you to the Hallamshire Hospital to get it reattached. And please don't swear. Nobody's here right now, but you shouldn't get into the habit of swearing."

Fred: "What are you doing up there, Irie? Any chance I can get you to come down and hold the wooden handle while I insert the shaft?"

Irie resisted the urge to throw the broken shoe at him. It was a great idea, actually. She turned to pick it up, but it wasn't there anymore. Just a few bits of broken wood. Splinters. No more than that.

Irie suddenly had a funny thought, and she just went ahead and said it out loud, "What would Dr Freud say about that request?" And then it dawned on her and on him that he was free. Or maybe he and she were trapped. But at least they were trapped together. An awkward silence followed.

Chapter 4

Exit from the Scythe Storage Room

Fred had a quick rejoinder for Irie: "Have you signed up to study Psychology in A Levels? Never too early to start reading. Maybe Freud's book on dreams. I can get you a copy from Waterstone's at Orchard Square." He, of course, had no idea that a dream (or something like it) figured so prominently in Irie's life right now. And he was only dimly aware of the sexual joke that Irie was making regarding the Sheffield steel shaft and its intended place in the wooden handle. And then there was the Swedish connection to Fred's last name. As for Irie, she suddenly found her witticism to be terribly embarrassing and wished she had kept her mouth shut.

So she said to him as a gesture towards their old back-and-forth way of conducting a conversation: "Nobody likes a smart ass." Those words, which he spoke to her the day before, were music to his ears.

Fred began to gush out his whole story: "Hey. It's so cool you showed up. First I was stuck in the train room. Then there was the green toilet. The big foot. A focaccia sammie, from you know who. Then I went down a long corridor. Another focaccia sammie. I was being fed. Then down the dumbwaiter . . ."

Irie interrupted, "So are you just going to stand around down there and play with rusty tools from 500 years ago, or are you going to come up here and buy me a cup of hot chocolate at the cafe?" She restrained herself from suggesting that he was well acquainted with the cafe, hot chocolate, and little bags of sugar. A girl should not get caught up too much in her imagination, or dreams, or whatever. Irie, like Lady Yerba, knew when to be a wise woman and when to keep her own counsel.

Fred had not seen the stairs. "Would love to. But I am stuck down here in this dungeon. It's like an oubliette. You know the places kings threw people they didn't like back in the Middle Ages. So, I'll need a rope. Is there a rope up there that you can lower down? I'll climb it like a monkey going after a coconut."

Irie was delighted to be hearing the old Freddie talk again about his favorite subject, England in the dark ages. "Oubliette"? What in the name of all that's sacred (and magical) is that? This she thought but went on to say: "Under that pile of junk over there are the stairs. But be careful. The steps may be rotten wood." And, of course, she didn't say "dark ages" because she knew it would wind him up. It was a good "trigger," as Americans of a certain sort were apt to say. Not that she had met any of them.

Fred decided on a gentle tease and quoted a line back to her that she often sent his way: "Why didn't you say so before? Now you tell me." Fred moved the wooden boxes of rusty hinges and the blocks of wood aside. There was even a big burlap sack full of shoes with wooden soles. Maybe safety shoes of the 1880s. All of this he cleared away and climbed the stairs. One step was definitely squishy, ready to give way under a heavy load. And then there they stood, the two of them separated by about six feet. They remained at this distance, not quite knowing what to do.

Irie, as always, had something to say: "Oh, Fred. You are so thoughtful. We are exactly two meters apart. Social distancing for COVID. My mother the nurse would be proud of you. But we are in a bubble and so safe with each other. Safe from one another." Again she suppressed her desire to say more, something about boys meeting up with strange year-13 girls for coffee or whatever. Even "safe from one another" was a slip, one of the Freudian variety.

Then, suddenly, the two of them ran at each other and hugged. Nobody started it. It just happened. AND their faces touched. Now the two of them had never actually hugged before. There was never an occasion for that sort of thing. They held together, face feeling face warmly, arms around one another. And just as quickly as that had happened it was gone. The two stepped back and looked like a couple of kids caught shoplifting chocolate frogs at a corner shop.

Fred spoke with the sort of shyness that he felt when asked to read poetry aloud in English class: "Merde! I don't have any money."

Irie found herself feeling completely calm, like Millhouses pond on a windless day with no RC boats in sight: "I do. Money is in you backpack, which I have right here. Change from bus fare that your mother gave you. Change from a tenner. The bus driver was going to kill you. Put you off the bus. He did not want to make change. Which would have been truly comic. If he had put you off the bus. Anyway, lots of change left over for hot chocolate. AND. I haven't heard that lovely French word in a while. 'Merde.' French is such a beautiful language. Quite reassuring, actually. Getting back to normal."

Fred: "Enough for a biscuit? I haven't eaten for awhile. I do have this two-litre bottle of water. Half full, as you can see."

Irie: "A cookie, Fred, a cookie. Try to talk like an American. Cookies come with the hot chocolate anyway. Do you like ginger snaps?"

Fred decided to be understated in his reply: "I could do with a ginger snap." The way he said this made him almost sound like he was doing a parody of Rafe.

Irie: "So when exactly did you last eat? You said you did, but when?"

Fred: "The last time was when I found a focaccia and the tart and a bottle of water in a cupboard in the county house kitchen. The stinking, low-down country house kitchen. I don't remember sleeping but I must have. Just a minute. There was a fainting couch. I might have slept on it. But I don't remember getting up in the morning. All I remember is walking down endless corridors until I reached a very old kitchen with gas lights. They weren't on, the gas lights. Probably not on for a hundred years. Anyway certain parts of my time in that place are erased from my memory. Maybe even the memory of time in that country house works differently."

Irie thought she would tease Fred just a tiny bit with an allusion to his words: "Find a sci-fi novel in the library of the stinking, low-down country-house?"

Fred ignored her little jest: "You know time is always a little funny once you've gone through Hobgoblin's gennel."

***

Irie and Fred were seated at the cafe table where she and the girl with the blue Hard Rock Cafe tee had sat earlier in the day. The lady from the counter had finished going through her receipts in the cash register and was sitting nearby in the almost empty cafe. The woman was going through her purse looking for something. Well, actually, she was doing a very good job of eavesdropping while taking sips from a cup of PG Tips tea with the wet tea bag sitting in an ash tray. This was odd, since none of the other tables had ash trays. And there was no smoking allowed in the cafe. In any event, Fred's appetite had returned with a vengeance and he was wolfing down a bacon sandwich. He was on his second cup of hot chocolate. Irie fiddled with a paper packet of sugar while considering the possibility of accidentally touching Fred's hand. She resisted the urge. For now.

Irie: "You could be in deep, deep trouble if Hobgoblin learns of the gusto with which you are chomping down that bacon butty."

Fred: "Why do people in Sheffield use that phrase for a couple of slices of bacon in a hamburger bun? Does it have to do with where the meat on the animal comes from?"

Irie pretended to be offended. "Freddie, please do not be gross. People might overhear you and not know that you are, in spite of your many failings, a perfectly nice young man." The lady from the counter appeared to have found what she was looking for, a packet of cigarettes. She rose and went outside to have a smoke.

When the lady could be seen outside sitting on a wall, cigarette in hand, Irie said, "Old people are so pathetic. And smokers . . ." At that moment the light slanting from the windows outside fell on Fred's right hand and Irie was sure she saw yellow stains. She spoke before she could stop herself, regretting what she said even as she said it: "Frederick Gustafson, what are those stains on your fingers? I saw you eyeing that woman's fags. Have you been smoking?"

Fred looked at her in disbelief: "You've got to be kidding, Irie. My grandfather in Yuma used to call them "coffin nails." Don's say "fags." That means something entirely different. And, for sake of clarification, no. The yellow on my fingers comes from the bits of leather in the boxes of machinery parts."

He had rescued her with a joke, and she rewarded him with a jest nestled in a false accusation: "Homophobe." They both burst out laughing. Neither one of them was that.

Irie: "You're still not safe from Hobgoblin. You need to feel some small revulsion while eating the bacon butty. You need to demonstrate loyalty." Both giggled. The lady from the counter came back in into the cafe.

Fred: "I'm a rebel. I owe allegiance to no man."

Irie: "Nor to no hobgoblin neither, it seems."

Fred: "Hobgoblin stuck me in that room with the trains. I simply could not get out."

Irie: "You stuck yourself in that room. With help from Orgone. . . I don't think you really tried to get out."

Fred: "Well not at first. But then I had to pee, and you know what?" Irie: "What?"

Fred: "There was a huge bathroom with a green toilet like the one at Lady Yerba's. And I had to pee and you know what happened next?"

Irie: "I actually do 'know what.' Or maybe I'm just not surprised. Let's go and thank Lady Yerba." Irie figured that it would be best if she didn't spill her knowledge of his story all at once. He could tell it. She could listen. She could compare the versions.

Fred: "Lady Yerba, again? Merde. Double merde."

Irie: "You owe it her. You know you do. But a word of advice. If she offers you a bowl of her menudo, politely refuse. Say you just ate a bacon butty. I doubt she'll be offended. She might even give you a dulce. She does a very nice peach in some sort of cream."

Fred: "You said something about Orgone. Did you find out anything more? Hobgoblin thought Orgone was going to try to hurt us. Emotions, something like that."

Irie: "I did pick up a little info on the topic of Orgone." Irie was not about to tell Fred what she was thinking, not right now, anyway. So, she just kept quiet and smiled a mysterious smile. Fred took out his cell phone. He looked at her frown and put it away.

All this time, Irie and Fred had their hands on the table, not far apart. It was his turn to fiddle with a packet, though it was a packet of pepper. He decided to put it back in its little white, ceramic cradle just at same time as Irie reached for the sugar. Neither consciously intended to touch the other but his fingers grazed the back of her hand. They both withdrew their hands, each with a certain sense of satisfaction. Neither was really embarrassed. Things had changed.

Chapter 5

Hoddy Dodd

Irie and Fred made their way to Lady Yerba's house taking the usual route. Fred, as might be expected, ran at the red pillar post box and swung around it. And up the driveway of Lady Yerba's they went, both stopping to tap the green toilet/cenote with the tips of their Converse sneakers. Fred, for a change, did not need to be told to tap. He was not ecstatically happy to do the bit with the toe of the shoe, but neither was he reluctant. There, as usual were the two red and black hens pecking and scratching in the long grass. Irie and Fred climbed the steps to the porch. Irie sat on the railing and Fred stood leaning against a post that supported the roof over where they were. The second aluminium lawn chair remained unoccupied. And then Irie remembered something. The snail. She wondered if it was there somewhere and looked around for it.

Lady Yerba saw what was going on. "She's not there, Irie. Hoddy Dodd."

Irie: "How sad. Just a snail, but still sad." Truth to tell, Irie was not sure why she was sad that the beautiful, yellow and black, whorled snail was not there. She wondered at her own interest. Although she had remembered Fred when she walked out of Hobgoblin's tall, green gennel, she had pretty much forgotten Nora. Not completely, but pretty much.

Lady Yerba repeated herself, "Not just a snail, Irie. Hoddy Dodd."

Irie began to get a sense of what Lady Yerba meant, but that sense was only beginning to emerge from a fog of memories. And then Irie said something that she would regret for the rest of her life: "Chickens like to eat snails. Maybe they got her."

Fred was not far behind Irie in saying something that he would soon regret: "My dad puts out beer traps for them. The snails drink the beer, get blasted, fall over, and drown."

Lady Yerba, who rarely showed strong emotion and who never lost her cool, became upset: "Both of you, don't say that. Mala suerte. Muy mala. Bad luck, very bad."

Fred: "Dad finally decided that it was a waste of good beer. Probably a waste of bad beer, since Dad always buys the cheap stuff. In Arizona it was Old Milwaukee. By the case."

Irie: "Freddie Gustafson, you need to have a little more respect. Do you want your kids to say things like that when you get to be a father?"

Fred: "It won't be a problem for me. I don't like the taste of beer. Dad once gave me a sip. Couldn't stand the stuff."

Irie and Lady Yerba looked at one another. Irie: "Do you want to say it or should I?"

Lady Yerba: "Go ahead, hija."

Irie: "Freddie boy, these words are going to come back to haunt you in five or six years. Maybe before. And I am going to be the spirit from another time who will say them to you. Wait and see." Fred did not press the point.

Now, Irie was still sitting on the porch rail facing Lady Yerba, and Fred was still standing leaning on the post that supported the porch roof. Both were looking at Lady Yerba, so they didn't see the girl with a blue jeans and the blue Hard Rock Cafe tee come sauntering up the driveway. Lady Yerba smiled and looked at the girl. Irie and Fred, sensing that someone was behind them, turned to look.

The girl spoke to Lady Yerba: "I don't know why you and Hobgoblin are so secretive about Hoddy Dodd. I mean, the two of you have a pile of secrets that make no sense at all."

Then the girl turned to Fred and said, "Long story short – the snail is your little sister, Fred. Nora, by name. Not the boffin older sister. The little kid."

Fred: "I don't have a little sister."

The girl: "You don't have a sister that you remember. And, Irie, you've definitely discussed this young member of Fred's family. Fred, you might have an excuse. Or you might not. Anyway, you both know now. Nora Gustafson, sister to Fred. Born in Yuma Arizona on a warm January day. There among the Gila monsters and the camper vans from Calgary. Irie, that's a city in Canada, as Fred will tell

186

you." Fred was quite fascinated to learn about his new sibling, his little sister now remembered.

Irie was furious, ready to take the aluminium lawn chair that was unoccupied and hurl it at the girl with full force. This girl had played little games with her about Fred at the Industrial Hamlet Cafe and was continuing to be obnoxious.

The girl: "Yes, your dream, Irie. Your fainting spell. That's where you learned about Nora."

Irie's anger cooled as she thought of how to put what she was going to ask. Finally, she said, "Not that I trust you to tell the truth, but was it a dream or something else? Something magical? Did any of it really happen? I'd really like to know."

The girl: "Maybe someday, when you are older, you and I can go for a cocktails and I will explain. You're still a little young yet." Irie looked daggers at the girl in blue.

For his part, Fred became perplexed in the extreme and his nose was definitely put out of joint. "Irie, in the name of your sacred Louise, what are you talking about?"

Now, Irie could not suppress a giggle and replied to Fred, "Oh you mean Jeez Louise." Then Irie turned to the girl and said, "But first, girl in the blue jeans and the blue Hard Rock Cafe tee shirt, Mr Sacre Vache and I would like to know your name. That's if you have one that you usually use and that we could rely on at least for the present conversation."

The girl: "I'm Flora, of course. I think you know my sister Florimell. She wears white all the time and really

187

knows how to get the boys at High Storrs School excited. Me, I'm the intellectual one in the family." At this remark, Irie giggled. Years later, as a mum with two lovely children at Totley school, she would say to her husband that she nearly wet herself at that moment. Intellectual? And the Hard Rock tee. What was that supposed to mean?

Irie turned back to Fred: "Flora the intellectual seems to have some sort of evil twin sister who visits people in their dreams. Visits people when those people are worried about other people. Worried sick to death. Flora's evil twin is a stupid busy body and pretty dumbass for a white-faced, idiotic, low-down temptress."

Fred appreciated the allusion to his phrase.

Lady Yerba interceded, "Florimell has some powers as a bruja. An English bruja, but not such a bad one. An actress/temptress, yes. Claro que sí."

Fred had no idea about what was being said but found himself uttering what the occasion seemed to call for: "A bit of a bruja." He paused and reformulated his witticism: "A bit of a blousy bruja."

Irie feigned disgust with what Fred's play on words: "Oh, Freddie. How could you at a time like this?" Flora, for her part, had no idea if Irie was genuinely unhappy with Fred.

Irie continued, "Mr Gustafson and I would like a little clarification. Was his younger sister, Nora Elizabeth Gustafson, turned into a snail by Hobgoblin for some offence against the goblin kitchen? Or by Lady Yerba for not finishing a bowl of magic menudo. Or by the great one, Orgone? Orgone himself for some yet-unknown reasons?"

Flora, who always liked verbal jousting, was delighted to respond: "You are fishing in the wrong pond, m'dear. The waters may be still and the RC boats departed, but there are no fish. No, I'm afraid it was the FQ herself who made that transformation. A royal personage that you have yet to meet. Should we try to arrange a visit. Hum, maybe 'audience' would be the better word."

Fred, however, was beginning to remember the details of living in a household that included Nora. He has not been paying attention to Flora. Fred: "You know, I do remember Nora now. She went to Greystones school. She was into fancy dresses. Pink unicorns. Ponies. And when we went to Bolsover Castle once, we couldn't get her out of the dress-up room. There were all of these costumes for kids to put on and mirrors for looking at yourself. English Heritage does a fine job for the little ones." Fortunately, he did not correct Irie about Nora's middle name which was Marian, after his mother's sister. Covering for a made-up detail in a story told by a pal is a true sign of friendship.

Flora: "And that's what got little Nora into trouble with Her Majesty. Into HM's wardrobe Nora goes. Examines the little dresses. Hangs them under her chin in front of the mirror. Tries one on. In comes the Fairy Queen in all her glory. At least the FQ turned Nora turned into a very pretty snail. A snail that few would forget. The sister might be forgotten, but the snail, no."

Irie found herself confronted with a major dilemma. She disliked Flora with a passion, but Flora held out the possibility of a visit to the Royal Palace, wherever that might be. A chance to see the Fairy Queen, herself.

While Irie was thus occupied pondering her next move, Flora casually observed all too casually as if it didn't matter: "But there's a way to restore the little girl to her little girl self. To get her to come out of her brightly painted shell."

Irie did not like this coyness about a serious subject: "OK, get on with it. What's the way to get Nora back to normal? The first, most important thing is to find Nora."

Flora resumed her teasing release of information: "Well, no. First you have to find the gold, garnet-encrusted drinking cup belonging to the Fairy Queen. If the cup is restored to its proper place, the girl will come right."

Irie was not sure about Flora's wording. "And be a girl again? I hope that's what 'come right' means."

Flora: "Yes and be a girl again. And be remembered by her family. One can offend the Fairy Queen, but later one can earn her gratitude. Or someone can act on your behalf. That's where you and Fred come in."

Irie: "So let's get down to nuts and bolts. What do we do next?"

Fred: "Yeah, we're sick and tired of getting the runaround on what to do."

Flora: "Oh come on. You should know by now that you'll need to figure this out yourselves."

Irie and Fred look at each other, sigh and say together: "Knew it." And then they said, also together: "Jinx."

Chapter 6

The Kitchen Tunnel Once More

The machinery of the grindstone room was running at full tilt when Irie and Fred opened the door from the outside. The leather belts and a set of three grindstones were creating a deafening racket. She and Fred quickly descended the steps to the scythe storage area, where it was a lot quieter. On the way down, Fred showed her the spongy step to be avoided, and, as they crossed the room itself, they stepped over various bits of junk on the floor. Irie carried Fred's backpack, from which protruded a water bottle.

Irie: "I hope you're right that the tunnel will lead us to the kitchen. Clearly this is our best chance to get back into the house. Maybe our only chance?"

Fred: "It's a slimy, filthy tunnel into that house. It's filled with snakes and toads and Gila monsters but it's a sure way in."

Irie: "Freddie Gustafson, stop it now."

Fred: "Do you think we should trust Flora? She's a pretty iffy character."

Irie: "Flora is a mark-one baggage and more than a little dodgy, but I don't think she's lying about us being able to find the Faerie Queen's cup. I have a feeling that the lot of them, Flora, Lady Yerba, and Hobgoblin are on our side and expect us to succeed. It's not going to be easy and that seems to be a part of the point. Maybe the main point. Here's how I see it: our method needs to be go with the flow, because we won't find the little lost royal item by sheer force of will. We can't plan this all out. And I really, really dislike the looks of that tunnel, so don't say that stuff again. But we have to free Nora whatever it takes. Buggah."

Fred: "I love it when you swear. It might the Lascar, seafaring blood in you. I can imagine you dressed in tight leather breeches like a pirate from Poldark. White billowing shirt and all." Fred realised that he had maybe gone a bit too far, so changed back to the topic at hand: "And we will free Nora. Definitely. Without a doubt."

Irie: "Yes, definitely we will free Nora." Irie paused, thought for a moment and said, "I trust Flora but she is creepy strange, and her twin sister, Florimell, is not OK. That Florimell, I wouldn't trust her in any of this. She cruises coffee shops looking for victims. If you're smart, you'll keep your distance."

If Irie was looking for a reaction from Fred, she was disappointed. He did not react to the thought that Florimell hung out in coffee shops or that there was any need for him to keep his distance. This would seem to confirm his innocence in Florimell's "not a boyfriend, yet" story told on the park bench. At the same time, Fred did not entirely miss the connection between himself and Florimell. And so the pair of friends, a little more than friends by now, peered into the kitchen tunnel. Dark as it was.

Irie: "This looks pretty dank and smells like a wet jumper that was left out in the rain overnight. Reminder: Don't go on about Gila monsters and other desert creatures, even if they could never live in there. Shall we take the dive?"

Fred: "There are little windows up at the top and that should help. But let's light it up. You're the one that likes to use the cell-phone flashlight."

Irie: "I am. I'm a lover of light."

Fred: "Let me remember." He paused and then: "There was some sort of tray on the tracks. And further along there's a track that's lifted up. A foot catcher."

Irie: "You said there was a trolley but not a torn up railroad. If I fall, I'll kill you." And on that cheery note, Irie and Fred entered the tunnel.

***

While Irie and Fred were entering the kitchen tunnel, Lady Yerba was positioned in her aluminium chair as usual. Flora was perched on the railing where Irie had been. Nora, the beautifully whorled, yellow and black snail, was contentedly munching dahlias.

Lady Yerba: "There are various ways into that house of the Inglés, but I believe the two young ones chose the safest. Sí. Creo que sí."

Flora: "It is huge country house. Hundreds of rooms. Some say 365 rooms in all."

Lady Yerba: "Much looking. The broom closets, the space under the stairs It could take them a while."

Flora: "Their families won't miss them and Nora seems pretty happy scoffing the dahlias. The danger is that those kids will get bored and come home empty handed, now that they know the way out."

Lady Yerba: "And don't forget Orgone and that danger."

***

When Irie and Fred emerged from the kitchen tunnel, he figured that he'd surprise her by taking the dumbwaiter up to the kitchen above. He climbed onto the wooden platform, found the rope, and gave it a little pull to test it.

As he adjusted himself on the platform Irie spoke, "I am not getting into that dumbwaiter thing. Do you actually know what you're doing?"

Fred: "It's fun, Irie. You just pull on the rope, and up the dumbwaiter goes." As he began to demonstrate how to pull the rope, there was a nasty-sounding creaking from above. He hastily jumped out, just before a pulley from above came dropping down and smashed into the platform where he had been sitting, splintering the wood. Fred and

Irie both quite at once realized that there were real dangers and they might not be ones that you would expect or could anticipate. Irie looked unsettled.

Fred: "More careful. More careful about everything. We need to be bold but not take stupid chances."

Irie: "You're not stupid."

Fred was pleased that did not say he was a fool, even if he felt like one. "Thanks. That gave me a fright, but thanks."

Irie put her head a little on one side, opened her eyes and said, "None of my friends are stupid."

Fred, having regained his composure corrected her grammar, "None of my friends is stupid." Both laughed.

Fred continued: "So, how are we going to get up to the kitchen?"

Irie: "We could take the stairs."

Fred: "Those stairs weren't here the last time. It's all changed."

Irie: "Maybe a good sign. And look at this staircase. It's nicely polished oak. And the colour is yellow, even gold."

Fred: "My dad had a golden oak desk in Yuma. It's that colour. Who polished it?" The house had changed in many ways since the two had first arrived there.

Irie and Fred quickly climbed the stairs and found themselves in a modern kitchen with no gas light pipes hanging overhead. And then Irie spied a set of French doors leading down the lawn to the garden. The doors were just at the beginning of the passageway with the pictures of the family. Men in stiff collars. Women in long white dresses. And little boys in sailor suits. She took Fred by the shoulders and pointed him towards what she had seen. Before the two friends was a large, beautiful patio that could be seen through the glass in the doors.

Fred: "Not much chance of going outside that way. I tried and it didn't work." Irie turned a door handle, which worked very nicely, and a light breeze from outside poured in on them. It was a lovely day. Sheer curtains waved gently in the kitchen windows. Down a well-mown lawn (no signs of sheep anywhere), could be seen a tidy pond in which paddled ducks and other waterfowl.

Fred was both charmed by the view and puzzled: "And I couldn't get outside last time. I was locked in. Locked in."

Irie: "Yes, that makes sense. Last time somebody wanted to keep you inside the house. This time, we are being invited to abandon our search. To wander down by the pond and watch the ducks. Then the sun will go down and we'll be stuck outside in the cold."

Fred: "Woa! Another temptation. Just like Sir Gawain." He thought for a second. "Hum, Sir Gawain's temptation was different. It was about a girl. But it is a temptation."

Irie: "Oh, Freddie. You and your pretty-boy Sir Gawain. Women tempting men, what a story. Let's go inside. But where do we start the search for the gold cup?"

Fred: "The drinks' cabinet."

Irie: "Bang on target. That would be hiding the precious object in plain sight. Just like a murder mystery."

Fred: "There will be a drinks cabinet in the library and another one in the billiard room. And about women tempting men, I thought you said that Florimell did that sort of stuff. I have yet to meet this friend of yours, but she sounds like a dangerous woman."

Irie was hugely relieved by what Fred was saying but tried to not be too gleeful. All she could manage for the moment was, "I guess so."

Fred: "And also a hidden stash in the bedroom of the lady of the house – if she's an alcoholic."

Irie: "Freddie!"

Fred: "A high probability in the English aristocracy."

And so the two retraced their steps from the sun-filled patio into the house in search of the Fairy Queen's gold cup, encrusted as it was with red garnets. Both were happy to have avoided the trap of going down to the pond, but just a tiny thought was wandering around Irie's brain – What if Fred Gustafson had been in the cafe with the horrible girl and had experienced the brushing of hands but forgot it. Had it removed from his memory only to be restored when the elfin F girl was ready to strike?

Chapter 7

Unguided Tour of an English Country House

Fred had a billiard cue in one hand and was spotting a ball on the green felt with the other. Irie was roosting on a high billiard chair observing. The room, like the rest of the house was well dusted and tidy, with magazines arranged neatly on a small table in one corner. The dates were all from May June of 1929. To one side on the table was a large glass ashtray. The billiard table was in immaculate condition, and a couple of men's flat caps hung on a hat rack. It was as if the household staff had finished its work in the room and left the gentlemen of an aristocratic family along with male friends to entertain themselves with billiards. That and conduct polite conversation about the decline of the empire and its chances of renewal. Fred bent his knees and looked down his cue, eyeing a shot.

Irie: "Freddie, please don't start playing a whole game of billiards. We've searched the drinks cabinet and all that was there was some scotch and brandy. And another thing. This house is now clean and spotless. Like new. New in 1920 something that is."

Fred continued to figure the angles: "It's an illusion. But let's shoot some pool before the spell is broken. Clearly another temptation designed to snare Gawain. He'd be passed out on the floor by now. He liked scotch whiskey. Pity we don't drink."

Irie: "Scotch wasn't invented back when Gawain was running around cutting off the heads of ugly green blokes. Would you please, stand up straight, turn around, put that billiard cue down, and listen to me?"

Fred: "Pool cue. There must be a jar of fresh cigars around here somewhere. It's part of the atmosphere. You don't have to smoke them. Just lay them in the ashtrays and pick them up from time to time. Call me Yuma Fats."

Irie: "Freddie, you're a caution."

Fred took his shot and dropped a ball into a side pocket. The problem that he faced was that the table was much larger than its American counterpart, and he had no idea about what rules applied. On the plus side, Irie was completely unaware of his abysmal knowledge of the rules that applied in an English country house. Irie was right, the billiard room was frozen in time in the 1920s, and on that account it was completely different from the modern kitchen that they had left several hours ago.

Irie: "We've pretty much searched everywhere and I'm getting tired of this game of find-the-gold-and-red-garnet-cup. Let's go back to the kitchen and see if anybody's left us anything to eat, like you said happened to you before. Maybe something other than a focaccia sandwich. We could do with a change of pace. Then knock off work and go home for the day."

Fred: "Me, I'll be happy with what I'm offered for chow. Focaccia is just fine. And what happens to you if Hobgoblin hears you say that you are getting bored with his deli service? Not something good, I think. I doubt you get to choose the animal you're turned into."

Irie was tired and hungry and wanted to go back to Sheffield. Fred could have stayed a while longer shooting a kind of billiards or pool that nobody had ever played.

Fred: "OK, you're right. Let's hit the kitchen and grab whatever's been left for us by whomever. And then home. But about what you said just a minute ago, That little jab: 'You're a caution.' That's from Little House on the Prairie. Are you secretly watching old bits of American TV?

And so they went off in the direction of the kitchen.

***

Irie and Fred did indeed find something to eat in the kitchen. The sandwiches were made on ciabatta, much to Irie's relief. She remembered that she hadn't said she didn't like focaccia. Just that she hoped for a change of pace. Any reasonable hipster hobgoblin would have understood. Perhaps the hobgoblin in him would have been tempted to turn her into a black and white magpie, but the hipster would have overruled that impulse. You simply cannot expect people to eat the same thing every time they show up in your deli. Or, in this case, open your kitchen cupboard.

Irie turned to see that the sun was casting long shadows on the lawn and when she opened the French doors to get a better view, there was no breeze at all. Just a warm afternoon cooling down. Fred knew that she was savouring the moment. The search was off at least for the day, and the two went outside.

Fred: "Let's go down there. Down to the pond. There's enough time before the sun sets. We can say "good-bye" to the ducks."

Irie: "FRED! I want to strangle you."

Fred: "You are so easy to take the Mickey."

Irie: "This is no joke. If we went down there now, night would fall in an instant and we'd be out in the cold. And 'take the Mickey.' That's not an American expression and it's dangerous to spout off English slang when you are in a haunted English country house."

Fred: "Haunted. Is that what it is?

***

It had indeed gotten dark quickly and Irie and Fred began to descend the steps leading to the kitchen tunnel. Fred took the bottle of water from the backpack.

Fred: "I think I'll have a slug of this. Unless you've drunk it all."

Irie: "Me? Little me?" She tilted her head to one side.

Fred lifted the bottle and looked at it. There was just about an inch left. He drank it all and put it back in the backpack.

Irie: "You didn't leave me any for me."

Fred shrugged his shoulders, turned, and walked over to the kitchen sink. The water ran clean, so he filled the bottle. And then he noticed it. The dishwasher. Something clicked in his head but he didn't know what it was, so he just handed Irie the water.

Fred: "A glass for madam? You know, we haven't searched this room." With that remark in mind the two quickly opened every cabinet in the kitchen. Irie found fresh bags of flour in one and looked behind them. Fred pulled out a spice drawer and set it on the kitchen table so that he could look in the back. They both came up empty handed.

Irie: "Mr Gustafson, would you be so good as to take me away from this place and to a world more suited to my upbringing?"

Fred: "Well, well, Miss Irie. We better get moving before the sun goes down." As they made their way back to the stairs, Fred looked over his shoulder and said, "I bet even the dishes in the dishwasher are clean."

Irie: "I bet it's empty."

Fred: "I guess we have to look if we are going to find out who knows the most about haunted country houses." And so the two sauntered over to the machine and Fred made an elegant bow to allow Irie to open it, which she did. There was nothing inside except for a gold, red-garnet covered drinking cup. Irie turned pale for an instant and then regained her composure.

Irie: "Mr Gustafson, may I have your opinion on the authenticity of this item?" For his part, Fred did a little dance. Then he joined into the unsympathetic parody of TV antiques shows.

Fred: "Has this gold, red-garnet-covered drinking vessel been in your family a long time?" First they laughed and then they went serious, suddenly realizing what the Fairy Queen did to Nora when Nora was messing about too much.

Both: "Better stop."

Both: "Jinx."

Irie: "You know what?"

Fred: "Nope. Tell me."

At this point Irie began to rummage around in Fred's backpack. First she took out a light rain cheater. Then Henry Sweet's Anglo-Saxon grammar. Finally out came the mahogany box with the crest that read MIR.

Irie: "But we don't want it to get damaged. I think it'll fit into my jewellery box."

Fred was partly joking and partly not when he said, "Your jewellery box? Klepto."

Irie emptied the contents of the box into a pocket in the backpack. Then, she compared the cup to the interior of the box." Irie: "Perfect fit. Like the box was made for it."

Irie placed the long-sought cup in the box and closed the lid. There was a sudden deep rumble in the house. Like a mild earthquake in Yuma. Cups jumped around on the shelves. Irie and Fred looked at one another and then the box slowly became fuzzy in their view, became fuzzy and disappeared altogether. More astounding than the mini earthquake was the shifting of images as the kitchen returned to its previous dusty state. There was no longer a dishwasher and yellowish-brown water was dripping gently from the tap over the sink. Again the two friends looked a one another. Fred was the one to turn off the tap all the way, for which action he was duly thanked by Irie.

Chapter 8

A Conversation with Lady Yerba

Irie and Fred, on their way to Lady Yerba's house, came upon the red pillar post box. Yes, that one. The one he always ran at and swung around. He didn't this time. Irie gave him a wry smile, and soon the two were trudging up the driveway, which seemed steeper than before. There they found Lady Yerba sitting in her aluminium chair and Flora situated on the railing. The sight of Flora caused Irie and Fred both to give a firm tap the cenote/toilet. They feared that this was not going to be a happy homecoming.

Irie spoke as if Flora weren't present: "Lady Yerba. We found it. The gold cup. But then we lost it. We were trying to transport it carefully using a mahogany box where it seemed to fit. And then the kitchen was hit by an almighty shaking. I hope the cup is not gone forever. Dissolved into who knows what."

Fred: "We didn't lose it, really. It disappeared on its own, and the whole house felt like it was going to come down on top of us. There are these big earthquakes that are centred in California and we get some of in Yuma. It was like . . ." Irie looked at Fred and he knew that there was no need to rattle on about Western Arizona.

Irie: "Freddie! That doesn't matter. We did lose it. We had it and then it was gone. Might as well take responsibility. Man up."

Fred: "Are you kidding me. Did you really say that? 'Man up.' I am deeply disappointed in you Miss Irie. Deeply, deeply." Sometimes it was difficult to take Irie seriously even in serious situations.

Getting the matter out in the open made Irie feel much better, relieved in fact. But it was at this point that an eight-year-old girl appeared from inside the house, where she had just procured for herself a handful of ginger snaps. She plunked herself down on the aluminium chair facing Lady Yerba and began munching cookies. Irie and Fred, who remained standing, had no idea who this small child was. Which is to say that he did not remember her. This forgetfulness did not last long. Slowly it dawned on him that she was his little sister. The child was Nora. She, of course, knew him and was aware of the existence of Irie, but that did not obligate her to say even a Yorkshire, "hiya." Nora remained silent, absorbed in thoughts of another world.

Lady Yerba: "The missing cup is now back with her highness. The spell on Nora is no longer applied. Mr Gustafson: "Quierro presentar su hermana.' I present to you your sister, Nora. I can see by the look on your face that you now are now remembering her."

207

Nora continued nibbling on the ginger snaps, which were encased in pairs in little cellophane wrappers, such as come with hot drinks at the Industrial Hamlet Cafe. Nora spoke to nobody in particular: "Queen Mab's closet is filled with these lovely clothes. And some of them fit me exactly. I got to meet her and she let me play anywhere in her palace. Queenie said I could. So, I did. We're best of friends. Besties, sort of." Now this little bit of childhood arrogance did not sit well with Irie.

Irie: "Queen Mab? You two are pals, besties? So tell me, what was it like being turned into a snail? Is that what 'besties' do to one another to show undying friendship? How did you like dodging chickens all day. Crawling around on your slimy stomach."

Now, Irie was not usually as unpleasant as she was just now. But she felt that she and Fred had taken some pretty big risks on behalf of his little sister. That little sister Nora was being horrid. And definitely was not showing any gratitude. No gratitude at all for what Irie and Fred had gone through. The falling pulley in the dumbwaiter, the lure of the dangerous duck pond. Nora didn't know or care to know.

Fred: "Long time, no see, sis. Did you enjoy life as a gastropod?"

Nora: "Still wearing that Yuma Criminals tee shirt. You should have mom give it a wash. And you can tell your girlfriend that living a snail's life is not a bad one. Not a lot of homework. Zero quizzes and exams. The chickens not a real danger. Lady Yerba keeps them off of the porch using some sort of magic. And she feeds them high-quality chicken food. If you're a snail, dahlias taste great. You should try them, but only if you've been turned into a snail."

Fred decided that it was time to be the big brother, to assume a little authority: "Don't you ever mess in that wardrobe again. Everyone forgot you. I wish I could say that your mother was worried sick. She wasn't because she forgot about you completely. Do you want her to forget about you? And what about your older sister? Without you to pester her, she only has Rafe. Waste-of-Space Rafe. She needs to lose that boy. And . . ."

Irie interrupted: "Fred! I think that's quite enough. Jeez Louise."

Fred: "If I may be permitted a last word – merde."

***

After the chat at Lady Yerba's, Irie and Fred went for a long walk. As they made their way through the tall, green gennel, they let the backs of their hands lightly drag through the conifers. Much passed through their minds, but at last they stood looking back at where they had been.

Fred: "We didn't drop in and see him. We sort of should have. It would have been polite."

Irie: "Yeah. Same with me. I really do like him. The little hipster. But not right now. And clearly you want to head for the RC boat pond before it gets dark."

Irie looked pensive and Fred replied, "If we went into that kitchen, he would give us another task to perform. Who knows, maybe we'd find ourselves sent to an abandoned World War II airfield. Lots of Spitfires and Hurricanes in bad repair. Maybe even an American P51 Mustang with the supercharged Merlin engine. If we didn't get killed by an unexploded bomb with a faulty fuse, then we'd emerge back in the world of Sheffield years later. Melanie would be married with kids. Not to Rafe, if there is any goodness in this world. And Sanka? He'd no doubt be head boy at High Stores School."

Irie: "Well, Mr Freddie, I sometimes do have the feeling that there are lost relatives wandering around Sheffield in the forms of all sorts of wildlife. I shall not elaborate on which."

And then Irie and Fred were at the stone bridge that had the inscription. Quickly they made their way down the slope to find that the place where the words had been. The place on the stone was covered with a new layer of moss. Irie scrubbed off the moss with a little smooth rock. Nothing. No words. Nothing.

Fred: "So, no inscription. No way back to see Hobgoblin. No focaccia, no ciabatta. No bitter orange tart…"

Irie smiled quietly and said, "Oh, I think there will be a word to chant. Maybe not like the last time, but a word."

Fred: "We could try the last one right now to see if it still functions, the "hw" sound. Hwath…"

Irie: "Freddie, if you say that, I will kill you. I've got a 95% confidence level that it won't work, but I'd rather not chance it. I want to stay in Sheffield for a while. It's home."

Fred: "Dorothy has Kansas. Irie has Sheffield – If you don't mind, we could look at the RC boats. We could wander over to the Millhouses pond. It all seems a little like kid stuff, though."

Irie: "Dorothy has Kansas. Irie has Sheffield. Freddie has Yuma. And, by the way, you're not a kid anymore. But I'll indulge you with the RC pond if we later can exchange stories about families while seated on our bench. You can tell me about the American Civil War battle of Gettytown and the Getty Museum."

Fred: "Don't be a major doofus. It's the battle of Gettysburg and the Getty is an art museum in Los Angeles. Is this another send up? If so, it fell on the floor."

Irie: "Major doofus?"

Fred: "My father sometimes says it to my mother."

The two of them then climbed the slippery clay bank of the brook, using tree roots as firm footholds. But they didn't walk on towards the pond or the bench right away. Fred had one last thing to say, before they left where they were – the stone bridge near the high, green gennel. And so it was that the two stood facing one another, each half sitting on the stone railings of the bridge.

Fred spoke first: "So if her majesty is named Mab, then there are sure to be red-pillar post boxes with the initials M and R in the realms that she rules."

211

Irie: "What are you talking about?"

Fred: "The red pillar post box. Elizabeth II Regina. We see it every time we go to Lady Yerba's. 'E' and 'R. With a Roman numeral two in the middle. You know, 'E' for Elizabeth. 'R' for 'Regina.' Queen Elizabeth. She who hangs her many floppy hats in Buckingham Palace."

A light bulb had turned on over Irie's head. Fred would later say that idea that had jumped out like the tongue of a Gila monster snagging a desert cricket. Irie spoke, "That's it. The mahogany box with the initials belonged to the first and only Queen Mab. The box. That was the queen's box. M for Mab. R for Regina. Queen. And a Roman numeral I in the middle. Queen Mab, the First. We put the gold, red-garnet covered cup into her box and the cup went home to her. It went home to her. That got Nora free."

Fred: "Good thing you didn't successfully steal the box. You'd be lord knows what sort of animal right now. If she transformed Nora into a snail for trying on clothes, what would Good Queen Mab do to someone who stole her mahogany box?"

Chapter 9

Park Bench under a Sessile Oak

Irie and Fred sat under the sessile oak on their favourite bench in Millhouses Park. There was only a scattering of people, which suited their sense of wanting to be off by themselves. That is off by themselves in Sheffield and not in an English country house full of illusions, interesting as that sort of experience could be. Perhaps the reason for there being so few people around was that there was a Sheffield United Football match at Bramall Lane. Down closer to town centre, there would be men and women in red and white striped shirts downing a last beer at the pub before entering the stadium. For his part, Fred no longer said "soccer" when he was with Irie. Indeed, he need to stop himself from saying "American football" when he was with Americans and talking about their favourite sport. He made no attempt to explain to English football fans why Americans call their game football, when the ball was mostly carried or thrown.

Fred: "I think I may change what I signed up for with A-Levels. The classes for the fall. The autumn. You know what I mean." He still went both ways with language.

Irie: "You're allowed make the shift in the courses you choose. Not too late even though its June."

Fred: "So here's what I'm thinking. I'm going to take classes in psychology. I'll do psychology as one of my three subjects. The other two – history and classics."

Irie was taken off guard. She had no sense that Fred had any interest in behavioural sciences. He liked history and things of a historical sort – which is to say classics.

Irie: "You have got to be kidding."

Fred: "I want to read Freud and study the libido and the id and maybe some of Freud's followers. So psychology but also the history of the subject. The subject in context."

Irie: "Orgone? Fears and desires? Not just history."

Fred: "For sure fears and desires. How can you have adventures without fears and desires? Also, I'd like to study developmental psychology. How kids grow up. How kids change as they get to be grown-ups."

Irie: "How kids get caught in the middle. Grown up enough to own a mobile phone but also grown up enough to be forced to keep the bedroom tidy. No freedom to be messy."

Fred: "And, of course, responsibility to do some chores in the family."

Irie: "Jeeze Louise."

Fred: "Like looking after a younger brother so that mum can go shopping without having to keep her eye on a wandering six-year-old."

Irie: "Now that might be going just a little bit too far. If we had done the babysitting for Sanka, you would have missed the trains in the country house. A formative experience for a young man. In addition, there was whatever happened in the grindstone room. The joys of the Industrial Hamlet cafe."

Fred did not get the allusions to Florimell.

Fred: "With freedom comes responsibility, or so they say. Hum. Sounds like merde to me."

Irie: "So, I had a little side conversation with Lady Yerba back when we were being introduced to Nora."

Fred: "And?"

Irie: "I need to go and dig some roots in a special part of the wood. A secret place. Want to come along?"

Fred: "Maybe, what's in it for me?"

Irie: "How about this?"

She handed him a little chocolate frog.